"Now I Have A New Wife And A New Business," Mike Replied.

"Not a real wife," Savannah said softly.

"A very real woman and one I want to get to know. I want to know what's beneath that cool control you always show to the world."

She smiled. "The trouble is you're too accustomed to getting your way."

"I won't get my way tonight."

"You're a dangerous man, Mike. I'm grateful to you for what you're doing, but I'm not giving you my body or my heart out of gratitude."

He cocked one dark brow. "Always a challenge from you, Savannah." He raised her hand and kissed her palm, slowly lingering.

"You know how I react to you. There's no hiding or changing it."

"And that makes you irresistible," he replied.

Dear Reader,

We're so glad you've chosen Silhouette Desire because we have a *lot* of wonderful—and sexy!—stories for you. The month starts to heat up with *The Boss Man's Fortune* by Kathryn Jensen. This fabulous boss/secretary novel is part of our ongoing continuity, DYNASTIES: THE DANFORTHS, and also reintroduces characters from another well-known family: The Fortunes. Things continue to simmer with Peggy Moreland's *The Last Good Man in Texas,* a fabulous continuation of her series THE TANNERS OF TEXAS.

More steamy stuff is heading your way with *Shut Up And Kiss Me* by Sara Orwig, as she starts off a new series, STALLION PASS: TEXAS KNIGHTS. (Watch for the series to continue next month in Silhouette Intimate Moments.) The always-compelling Laura Wright is back with a hot-blooded Native American hero in *Redwolf's Woman. Storm of Seduction* by Cindy Gerard will surely fire up your hormones with an alpha male hero out of your wildest fantasies. And Margaret Allison makes her Silhouette Desire debut with *At Any Price,* a book about sweet revenge that is almost too hot to handle!

And, as summer approaches, we'll have more scorching love stories for you—guaranteed to satisfy your every Silhouette Desire!

Happy reading,

Melissa Jeglinski

Melissa Jeglinski
Senior Editor, Silhouette Desire

Please address questions and book requests to:
Silhouette Reader Service
U.S.: 3010 Walden Ave., P.O. Box 1325, Buffalo, NY 14269
Canadian: P.O. Box 609, Fort Erie, Ont. L2A 5X3

SHUT UP AND KISS ME

SARA ORWIG

Published by Silhouette Books
America's Publisher of Contemporary Romance

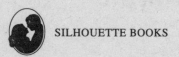 SILHOUETTE BOOKS

ISBN 0-373-76581-9

SHUT UP AND KISS ME

Books by Sara Orwig

Silhouette Desire

Falcon's Lair #938
The Bride's Choice #1019
A Baby for Mommy #1060
Babes in Arms #1094
Her Torrid Temporary Marriage #1125
The Consummate Cowboy #1164
The Cowboy's Seductive Proposal #1192
World's Most Eligible Texan #1346
Cowboy's Secret Child #1368
The Playboy Meets His Match #1438
Cowboy's Special Woman #1449
*Do You Take This Enemy? #1476
*The Rancher, the Baby & the Nanny #1486
Entangled with a Texan #1547
†Shut Up and Kiss Me #1581

Silhouette Intimate Moments

Hide in Plain Sight #679
Galahad in Blue Jeans #971
*One Tough Cowboy #1192

*Stallion Pass
†Stallion Pass: Texas Knights

SARA ORWIG

lives in Oklahoma. She has a patient husband who will take her on research trips anywhere from big cities to old forts. She is an avid collector of Western history books. With a master's degree in English, Sara writes historical romance, mainstream fiction and contemporary romance. Books are beloved treasures that take Sara to magical worlds, and she loves both reading and writing them.

One

What other weird thing will Special Forces get me into? Michael Remington wondered as he glanced around the elegant law office that was located on the main street of San Antonio, Texas.

Dark wood walls, polished oak floor, comfortable leather chairs, and the attorney the most decorative part of all. He looked at her silky blond hair, hair that shouldn't be confined in the twist at the back of her head. From the first few moments, when she'd stood in front of her desk, he'd noticed that the lady had fabulous long legs. Besides her legs, she had a face and figure that made a man think of the bedroom—until he looked into her big blue eyes, cold and icy as a Nordic fjord.

He barely listened while she waded through legalese, reading John Frates's will. Mike's best buddies from Special Forces were seated beside him: tough Jonah Whitewolf, a Comanche, one of the best bomb experts Mike had ever known; and next to him, Boone Devlin, chopper pilot deluxe.

Not long after their rescue of John Frates, the three of them had been split up, and they hadn't seen one another until today, the first week of April. Mike was looking forward to their dinner together tonight. A reunion would be a blast, and they could thank John Frates for accomplishing the get-together. Only, John Frates and his wife were no longer living—both had died in a boating accident off the coast of Scotland. It was odd as hell to get remembered in a will simply because you did your job, Mike thought. They had rescued John Frates when he was held hostage in a Colombian jungle, but it had all been part of the mission.

When he heard his name read, Mike's attention returned to the attorney. She was a looker, but the minute he'd walked into her office, they'd clashed. Although he knew there were plenty of female attorneys, he had assumed from her letter, signed S. T. Clay, that she was male. But S. T. Clay was very much female and she had resented his mistaken assumption. If it meant that much to her, she should sign her letters as Savannah Clay. There was no wedding ring on her finger, and Mike wasn't surprised. She might be gorgeous, but she was none too friendly.

"'To Michael Remington,'" the attorney read in her brisk, no-nonsense voice, "'to whom I shall be forever indebted, I leave my most precious possession, the guardianship of my baby daughter, Jessie Lou Frates.'"

A jolt shot through Mike with the impact of a current of electricity. Stunned, he stared at Savannah Clay. He couldn't get his breath, he broke out in a sweat, his ears began to ring and he was unable to hear anything else she said.

Jessie Lou Frates? A *baby?* He was bequeathed the care of a baby girl? John Frates had called him about a will, but he hadn't said anything about a baby. As far as Mike knew, there hadn't been a baby at the time John called him.

Mike knew absolutely nothing about babies. He'd never

wanted to be tied down that way. In his military career he had been through all sorts of life-or-death situations, and he had never felt as light-headed or as nervous as he was right now.

He barely heard the rest of the reading of the will, nor the questions the others asked when it was done. Finally Savannah Clay looked at him.

"You're very quiet, Colonel Remington. Any questions?"

He gazed into those crystal-blue eyes—fabulous eyes, he thought fleetingly. "Yes, I have a lot of questions. If you have a few moments, I'll stay when the others leave so I don't take up their time."

The guys protested, but with a wave of her hand Miss Clay silenced them.

It was another thirty minutes before she closed the door behind them and turned to him. When she did, he rose to his feet to face her across the office.

"I'm not taking any baby," Mike declared. "John Frates never said anything about a baby."

"I understood that he did call you," she replied smoothly.

"Several years ago he called me and said he had recently married and they were writing wills and he wanted to leave something to me, but he didn't say one thing about a child," Mike repeated stubbornly.

Savannah Clay studied Mike with a look that made him think she didn't believe him. "When Jessie was born, John and his wife rewrote their first wills." The attorney crossed the room to return to the seat behind her desk, and in spite of the shock he'd just received, Mike could not help noticing the sexy sway of her hips as she walked. She motioned to him. "Please sit down."

"I can't be responsible for a baby," Mike repeated, wondering how long it would take to get through to her.

"You'll be completely provided for by this will. You'll have the Stallion Pass house, a trust fund for Jessie, a trust for daily living and a million and a third dollars goes into your account tomorrow,'' she replied as if explaining something simple to a small child.

''Don't put anything into my account,'' Mike snapped. ''Aren't you listening? I'm *not* becoming a guardian to this child.''

''The Frateses don't have any relatives,'' Savannah stated. ''There is no one else to take her. She's only five months old.'' The color that heightened her cheeks only added to the good looks he was trying to ignore. She spoke slowly and firmly, as though he was hard of hearing or just too dense to get what she was trying to explain to him. ''She'll become a ward of the state otherwise.''

''I'm sorry, but she'll have to become a ward of the state,'' he replied tersely. ''It doesn't change how I feel. There are a lot of children out there that are wards of the state, but I'm not taking any of *them,* either.''

Fire flashed in the depths of blue ice as Savannah's eyes narrowed. ''John Frates had the very highest opinion of you, and he placed his faith and trust in you. He praised you beyond measure.''

''That's certainly flattering, and I appreciate his opinion, but the guy was grateful because we rescued him. It doesn't change my decision.'' Mike's tone was forceful.

''Look at this.'' She shuffled through papers and yanked out an envelope, then came around the desk. She turned a chair and moved close beside him, and he caught a whiff of enticing perfume. When she crossed her legs, his attention was briefly distracted, caught and held momentarily by her long, shapely legs.

Savannah pulled out a picture and placed it on his knee, and the slight contact caused a different kind of jolt, one that settled in a region below his belt. ''This is Jessie,'' Savannah said.

He looked at a picture of a smiling, dimpled baby with

curly ringlets of black hair, twinkling blue eyes and rosy cheeks.

"She's adorable, but I'm *not* changing my mind."

"May I ask why?" Savannah twisted to face him. Their knees were almost touching, and he was aware of her as a very appealing woman, if an annoying one.

"I'm single. I value my freedom and I don't know anything about kids," he replied.

"Maybe it's time you learned."

His annoyance rose a notch. "No, this isn't the right time for a baby in my life. I'm getting ready to join the CIA. I'll be traveling. I can't be encumbered with a baby."

Her eyes narrowed. "That's incredibly selfish of you, Colonel Remington. You're turning down a generous income, a home, a precious baby, simply because you value your freedom?"

"You're getting it now," he said. The woman had the bluest eyes he'd ever seen and the most fabulous legs. And he couldn't wait to get away from her and this unwanted legacy.

"Have you already joined the CIA?" she asked.

"Not yet, but that's beside the point."

"You're single. Is there a woman in your life?" she persisted.

"Not at the moment."

"I'm not surprised," she said coolly, and Michael's temper boiled over.

"Look, Miss Clay, you're not exactly a bundle of warmth yourself. Obviously you're single, and I'm not surprised by that, either."

To his amazement, she laughed. Beautiful white teeth, a sparkle in her eyes. More appealing than ever. He wanted to gnash his teeth. Attila the Hun packaged as an alluring woman. "Ah, I'm getting to you," she said with cheerful satisfaction. "You're losing that cool control. It means your guilty conscience is at work."

"It means no such thing," he said, watching her dazzling smile. It took his breath away.

Glancing at her watch, she said, "It's late. Come have a drink and dinner with me, and we can discuss this issue further," she announced, standing.

"No thanks," he replied as she shed her suit jacket, unclipped her hair and shook her head. Blond hair cascaded over her shoulders and fell onto a creamy silk blouse clinging to curves that made him momentarily forget his animosity. She had a waist he could easily span with both hands.

"Do you often turn down a woman's invitation for a dinner date? Or are you scared I might win you over to my way of thinking?" Savannah asked him.

He arched an eyebrow and wanted to give that cute fanny a swat. If he had any sense, he would answer yes and get the hell out of her office and life. But she was standing there with golden hair falling over her shoulders, a challenging gleam in her blue eyes and a figure that would make most men forget all the problems in the world.

"No, I don't turn down offers from beautiful women," he said quietly, standing and placing his hands on his hips. "I'm not scared, but you'll never win me over to your way of thinking on this."

"Never is a long time, Colonel."

"All right, since we're going to dinner, let's drop the formalities. It's Mike, Savannah."

"Fine," she said, granting him another one of her dazzling smiles. "Sit down, Mike. I'll only be a few minutes."

She gave orders as casually as a drill sergeant. Far more polite, but with that same authority and absolute expectation of being obeyed. Mike walked around the office, not really curious about the place, but simply being obstinate because she had told him to sit. As she disappeared through the door, he glimpsed a leather sofa and a wet bar. She must have a very successful practice.

While he studied a painting, he called the hotel where he and his two buddies were staying to talk to Boone. "I need to talk to this attorney tonight about my inheritance," he told him, "and I'm going to have to cancel our dinner. This is crazy. I can't deal with a baby."

"You looked like you'd been shot," Boone said.

"I felt like it," Mike admitted.

"I think all three of us are a little in shock, Mike. None of us expected this. Let's get together another time—how about breakfast, eight o'clock, hotel restaurant?"

"Great," Mike replied. "See you then. Tell Jonah for me, would you."

"Sure."

Shutting off his phone, Mike continued to stroll around Savannah's office, reading the spines of the law books lining the shelves, studying oil paintings of seascapes and all the while remembering the first few moments of his arrival. A few hours ago, he had entered the one-story brick building with gold lettering over the doors that read Slocum and Clay, Attorneys at Law.

Mike had walked through the front doors into a spacious waiting room and told the attractive brunette receptionist that he had an appointment with S. T. Clay. She had told him to go right in, that he was expected and it was the first door on the right.

He had walked down the hall to the door, knocked lightly and went inside. The tall blonde that turned to face him had smiled. Her blue eyes were riveting, the color of tropical seas.

"Excuse me, I'm looking for the office of S. T. Clay. Are you his secretary?"

"I'm S. T. Clay," she replied, crossing the room and extending her hand. "Savannah Clay."

His brows arched. "Oh. I expected a man."

"Instead, you've got a woman," she replied coolly. "And you must be Colonel Remington."

"How'd you guess?" he asked, tilting his head slightly.

"John Frates gave me brief descriptions of all of you. He said you were a direct, take-charge type."

Mike could feel a clash of wills already. He shook her hand. He expected a hard grip, and she didn't disappoint him.

"I've been direct," he replied quietly, amused. "I don't think I've begun to take charge yet."

"And you won't in my office," she replied just as quietly, giving him a faint smile, and again he experienced the silent clash of wills. "Please be seated. I'll be with you in a moment." She'd left the room and he'd walked to one of the leather chairs, thinking that he could tell the lady a bit about herself from this first encounter. He suspected no one was more of a take-charge type than she was....

Mike brought himself out of his reverie, knowing that from the first he'd gotten off on the wrong foot with the woman. Still, the evening might be interesting. He wondered if kissing her would be like kissing an ice sculpture...or was there a real woman there beneath the ice?

You'll never know, he told himself silently.

And then Savannah returned and he rose to his feet, his recollections forgotten. "Sorry to take so long. I had to make a few calls," she said. They left her office. As they walked through the hallway, a tall, blond, deeply tanned man stepped from his office with an attractive redheaded woman beside him.

"Troy, Liz, I'm taking a client to dinner," Savannah said. "This is Colonel Remington. Mike, this is my partner, Troy Slocum, and one of our associates, Liz Fenton."

Mike shook hands with them both. Troy Slocum, dressed in a dark blue suit and exuding success and self-confidence, said, "So you're the fantastic Colonel Remington, the man John Frates thought so much of."

"I don't believe 'fantastic' fits, but that happens sometimes when you save someone's life. I was only doing my job,'' Mike replied, slightly wary of Troy. He wondered why, since he had never met the man before. But his instincts were seldom wrong.

"If you two will excuse us, Liz and I have a conference call," Troy said abruptly.

Savannah and Mike said goodbye and turned away.

"Did I do something to him?" Mike asked.

"Pay no attention to Troy. Even though he has no reason to be, he's jealous of other people's success."

"How many partners and associates?" Mike asked, dismissing the incident from his mind as they walked to the door.

"Troy is my only partner, and we have one other associate besides Liz—Nathan Williams."

Enjoying watching Savannah, Mike followed her out and motioned toward the rental car he was driving.

"I'll drive," she said, jingling keys. "I know where we're going."

He wondered if she was going to rush ahead and hold the car door for him, but she didn't. While he held *her* door, she slid inside, giving him another glimpse of shapely legs. He went around and slid into the passenger seat.

"Tell me about your life, Colonel," she said after they had turned into the street.

"Mike, remember?"

"Mike, tell me about your life."

"I recently got out of the military, so my life is changing. I suspect you already know some things about me."

"Right. You're thirty-six, born in Montana and went to the Air Force Academy before joining the military. You're single, very smart. You have a younger brother, Sam, who lives in San Jose. You have another younger brother, Jake, who lives in West Texas. Your parents have moved to California. That's about it. Your history leaves lots of blanks."

"Not so many," he said, turning to watch her drive. To the eye she was a gorgeous babe, but the moment she opened her mouth, the lawyer was revealed, and what was really beneath all that pretty packaging—an aggressive, tough, no-nonsense woman.

She drove fast and competently with her window open and the wind blowing her golden hair. She knew he was watching her, but it evidently didn't disturb her. What was it between them that made the sparks fly? That made him feel repelled and attracted at the same time?

"So, how about you tell me about you, Savannah? I don't know anything, except you're the Frateses' attorney."

"I went to Stanford for my undergraduate degree, and then to Texas University for my law degree. I have three brothers and three sisters."

"A big family."

"I suppose we are," she replied.

"And you're the oldest?"

She smiled and shook her head. "Why did you guess oldest?"

"You're a take-charge type."

"Actually, I'm the fourth child. I'm was born in Stallion Pass."

"The same place John Frates is from," Mike said.

"That's right. That's how I knew him," she said, growing quiet while she concentrated on driving. In minutes they parked and entered a restaurant with checkered tablecloths, candles on the tables and the smell of fresh-baked bread filling the air. "I should have asked—do you like Italian?"

"Of course," he answered as he held her chair.

When they were seated and had given their dinner orders, Mike studied her. "Now, tell me more about you and Stallion Pass, Texas. You don't seem like the small-town type."

"I'm very much the small-town type. I love Stallion Pass. John Frates's family businesses have really made Stallion Pass the town it is. Well, there are other businesses and families that contribute to it, but the Frateses did a lot. He had the oil company, Frates Oil, which he sold last year.

He remained as CEO so they will simply replace him, and that wasn't part of the will. He had the home that you received, the quarter-horse ranch and the cattle ranch—''

''Two ranches?''

She gave him a quizzical look. ''Didn't you listen as I read the will?''

''Actually, no,'' Mike admitted. ''After you announced I was inheriting a kid, I went into shock and didn't hear anything more you read. I wouldn't even think that kind of thing's legal.''

''Of course it's legal to appoint a guardian. John might not have told you about it, but I know he intended to.''

''Well, tell me what the other guys got, then. Did it occur to you that one of them might take little Jessie?''

''We'll get to that,'' she said, her cool, I'm-in-charge voice returning. ''Jonah Whitewolf got the cattle ranch. He can do with it whatever he wants—sell it, keep it or lease it.''

''I'd guess Jonah will sell it. John Frates should have discussed all this with us in more detail.''

''I don't think he dreamed that anything would happen to both him and his wife. Boone Devlin inherits the quarter-horse ranch—it's famous nationwide for its horses.''

Mike shook his head. ''Boone and a horse ranch. He grew up on a farm and wanted to get away from it. The flyboy is nuts about planes. He won't leave his air-charter service. John Frates should have talked to all of us and talked to others who would have been better choices for these inheritances.''

''Once again, you're making snap judgments.''

''Maybe, but I know these guys as well as I know myself. We knew Frates was worth a lot, but not this much.''

''The Frates family was enormously wealthy, and when John sold the oil company, he received a lot more.'' She leaned forward, candlelight flickering in the depths of her eyes. For an instant, Mike was drowning in blue. His gaze lowered to her mouth, and he wondered if there was a woman beneath all that pushy, do-it-my-way exterior. What was she like in a man's arms? He leaned closer.

"Ever been in love, Counselor?"

If the question surprised her, she hid it well. She gave him a smile. "Maybe once in college, but not since."

"No steady guy now?"

"No," she replied, looking amused. "Going to ask me for a date?"

He smiled at her, and they both laughed. "I didn't think so," she said. She caught his wrist and the touch was electrifying to him. He took a deep breath, surprised at his reaction.

"Tell me something."

"Whatever you want to know," he said in a husky voice, beginning to wonder what it would be like to have a real date with her.

Those blue eyes nailed him. "If John Frates had called you and asked if you would be little Jessie's guardian, what answer would you have given him?"

Startled, all Mike's erotic thoughts vanished. He was staring into eyes that probed, accused and demanded an answer. What if John Frates *had* called and asked him to take his baby?

"I can't answer that, because he didn't call," Mike replied.

"You *won't* answer my question because if her father had called and asked you, you would have agreed to become her guardian," Savannah said in a voice dripping with satisfaction.

"I damn well would *not* have," he snapped, moving his wrist away from her grasp and leaning back in his chair. "Don't put words in my mouth. Are you a trial lawyer?"

"Occasionally," she answered, and Mike could imagine her nailing a witness and using that same satisfied tone. She looked down at her purse and whipped out the picture again.

"Look at this little baby. How can you refuse? You would have all the money in the world and could hire five nannies for her if you wanted."

"You think a dad who hands a baby over to nannies all the time is better than a foster home?"

"Yes! In foster care, she'd be shuffled around. If you had her, you'd care and you'd be responsible," Savannah answered heatedly, her eyes flashing. "Underneath that selfish exterior, there must be *some* heart—John saw that in you. I've known John all my life, and he was a good man and a very smart man. He didn't misjudge people."

"Give it up, Counselor. I'm *not* taking that baby," Mike replied, wondering how many times he was going to have to refuse.

Savannah put away the picture and leaned back while he drank some wine. He wished he had ordered something stronger. When their dinners came, he ate golden, cheese-covered lasagna in silence, thankful she had stopped badgering him but still annoyed with her for calling him selfish.

As soon as they finished, she picked up the check and drove him to his hotel.

"You gave it your best shot," he said before he stepped out of the car. "Sorry, but you can do something else with that inheritance."

"It's not that simple. Can you come by my office in the morning while we work out details?"

"Sure." He sat staring at her, thinking she was a beautiful woman sitting only a couple of feet away. His gaze dropped to her mouth, but he knew better than to try a kiss. "Night, Counselor."

"I don't know how you'll be able to sleep, or even look at yourself in the mirror."

"I'll sleep just fine, thank you. Do you always butt into people's lives like this?" he asked.

"Of course not—this is a big exception," she said, studying him intently. "I still think John saw something in you that I'm not seeing."

"I hauled his ass out of the jungle—it was a job. The man was grateful to have his life back, but gratitude can blind people."

"Not John. He told me about spending weeks with you guys because the escape didn't go as planned. He said that, in the life-threatening circumstances all of you were in, you really get to know someone. He said he knew he could depend on you completely."

"Well, too bad he's not here to know how much I've let him down. Good night and start thinking of someone else for that particular inheritance."

He climbed out of the car and closed the door, leaning down to speak to her through the open window. "Thanks for dinner."

She glared at him, put the car in gear and drove away. He stared after her and still wondered what it would be like to kiss her. His flight back to D.C. didn't leave until three o'clock tomorrow afternoon, but when it did, he would be on it, and he wasn't coming back to Stallion Pass or San Antonio, Texas, again. He had to see the lady lawyer one more time and then it was goodbye forever.

Savannah took a deep breath, exhaling slowly and trying to cool her anger. "Stubborn, selfish man!" she snarled aloud, gritting her teeth and thinking about the adorable little five-month-old girl who needed a guardian. Savannah glanced in her rearview mirror and saw Mike Remington walking into his hotel. Too handsome for words. She hated to acknowledge that, but he exuded sex appeal with his rugged good looks, raven hair and thickly lashed, dark-brown bedroom eyes. He had too much confidence, and she suspected he was accustomed to having women melt whenever he was around. A few times tonight when they'd touched, she'd hated that she'd gone all tingly; she hoped she'd been able to hide it well. She didn't want him to make her tingly.

She wished to remain aloof and frosty with him, so why hadn't she?

There had to be a way to persuade Mike Remington to take Jessie. John Frates was never off the mark in his assessment of other people—not like this. John had seen something in the man that had made him think Mike was the right man to take responsibility for little Jessie.

Whatever John had seen, Savannah knew she wasn't finding it. Mike Remington seemed almost hostile, and totally wrapped up in himself and his own life. He wasn't going to be charitable or generous. And he was going to walk away from a million-dollars-plus inheritance. What kind of man did that? She couldn't figure him out at all. She knew what John had said about him—that he was tough, fearless and intelligent. Now she could add selfish and stubborn to the list. Yet, how many truly selfish people would pass on a million and a third dollars?

Of the three men in her office this afternoon, Mike Remington seemed the *least* likely man to be the guardian of a child.

Maybe when Mike slept on it, he would change his mind. She knew better than to really believe that, though.

Savannah drove to the redbrick condo she owned in San Antonio. On weekends she went home to Stallion Pass, but during the week, it was easier to stay in the city.

She parked in her garage and entered through the back door, going in the short entryway to her kitchen. As she got herself a glass of water, she paced around her empty, lonely kitchen. She finally set her empty glass on the tile counter and went through the living room to her bedroom. As she readied herself for bed, her mind was still on Mike Remington. She couldn't seem to get him or the problem out of her thoughts.

An hour later she sat up in a rumpled bed, staring into the dark and still thinking about Mike and Jessie. She had been conscious of Mike as an attractive man from the start.

When she'd touched him, she'd felt the shock of that contact to her toes. She suspected he had that effect on most females.

She'd told him she needed to see him again, but that had been desperation talking. She prayed she could get the state caseworker to cooperate tomorrow. Surely there was some way to melt Mike Remington's hard heart.

As Savannah sat there in the dark, she was chilled by a deep, unsettling hurt that she hadn't experienced in years, and she knew what was making her fight so hard for little Jessie.

She recalled her family, her mother and father, her six siblings. All of them, except the three youngest children, were adopted. When she was four, her blood father had walked out. Then when she was five, her mother had abandoned her, as well, sending her to a neighbor's house and not coming back for her. That old hurt had dimmed, but she could remember the incredible pain and panic, the shock. The number of foster families she had been shuffled through for more than a year and a half—until Amy and Matt had adopted her and taken her into an unbelievably warm and loving home. Savannah shivered and rubbed her arms until old fears and hurts vanished.

In spite of trying to put Jessie and Colonel Remington out of her mind, Savannah slept little and was up before the sun.

Bathed and dressed for work by eight o'clock, she studied herself in the mirror as she smoothed her navy suit. She wore simple pearl earrings and a pearl necklace. Her hair was in a twist on her head. She thought she looked quite businesslike. Her thoughts jumped to Mike and the way he'd looked at her yesterday when she'd taken her hair down and removed her suit jacket. Her pulse jumped at the memory and she frowned, shaking her head. Glancing at the clock, she rushed to the phone to call the caseworker. Savannah knew it was only two hours till her appointment with Mike Remington. This would be her last chance with him, so she needed to make it count.

Two

Mike showered, dressed in a navy sport shirt and jeans, then went downstairs to meet his friends in the hotel lobby. He spotted the two tall men the instant he stepped out of the elevator. After greeting one another, they went to the hotel restaurant for breakfast. It wasn't until they'd ordered that the talk turned to their respective legacies, Mike's in particular.

"So how's it feel to suddenly become a father?" Jonah asked.

Mike shook his head and met Jonah's gaze squarely. "I'm not going to do it."

"You're turning down your bequest?" Boone asked in disbelief.

"I can't take care of a baby," Mike said. "Maybe one of you guys?"

"What? Swap inheritances?" Boone's eyes danced with amusement. "I don't think the lady lawyer would go for that. She's all business."

"She's as tough as my dad," Jonah remarked dryly. "No messing with her."

"Well, count me out, anyway," Boone said as he leaned back in his seat. "I've been there and done that with my kid brothers and sisters. No thank you."

"Boone, you're the oldest of nine. You'd be perfect."

"The hell you say!" Boone snapped. "No more changing diapers for me. I've been a daddy eight times. Forget it."

"How about you?" Mike asked, looking at Jonah.

Jonah shook his head. "I'm going home to Oklahoma, and from there I've got to go overseas in four days. Besides, the thought of a ranch is kinda intriguing."

"What do you know about ranching?" Boone teased. "Next to nothing."

"Not exactly. My granddaddy had a ranch and I lived with him off and on when I was a kid. Besides, ranching runs in my Comanche blood," Jonah replied with a grin of his own.

"Oh, sure," Boone said with a brief laugh, shifting his attention back to Mike. "Looks like you're stuck, pal. Sorry."

"I'll get out of it," Mike said grimly, more of a promise to himself than his buddies.

"And give up all that money?"

"The money's not worth it. I'll make my own money."

The waiter brought their breakfasts, and Mike looked at his friends. Jonah was the same as the last time Mike had seen him, except it was only April and already the sun had darkened his skin considerably. His straight black hair was cut short and neatly combed, and the T-shirt he wore revealed powerful muscles, proving that Jonah was still in top physical form. As for Boone, his skin was darkened, too, by the sun, and gone was his shaggy brown hair. Although still thick and wavy, it had been trimmed considerably, well above his collar.

"Where are you working now, Jonah?"

"Okmulgee Oil. I'm two weeks in an Algerian oilfield, two weeks home."

"So you're finally using that engineering degree," Boone said.

"I used it in the military. Engineering is a good background for defusing bombs. Better than a marketing degree. So what are you doing, Boone?" Jonah asked.

Boone grinned. "I live about twenty miles out of Kansas City, Missouri, and have my own charter service. I fly everywhere and anywhere."

"You couldn't give it up, could you," Jonah said. "Are you still in, Mike?"

"Nope. I got out two months ago. I've got an offer from the CIA and I plan to take it. I'm living in D.C. now. So, is anybody married?"

His two buddies looked at each other, but Mike saw the flash of pain in Jonah's eyes and guessed that he still hadn't gotten over his divorce. His marriage had ended while they were all in the service together.

"Remember that night in Fort Lauderdale?" Boone said to break the sudden pall in the mood, and in minutes they were reminiscing about those times. They continued until Mike realized he would have to hurry to make his ten-o'clock appointment with Savannah Clay.

"Guys, I gotta run."

"I'll get the check. I certainly can afford it with my new-found fortune," Boone announced. "The famous quarter-horse ranch that I intend to sell."

"Thanks, Boone." Mike pulled out a card. "Here's my address in D.C. and my home and cell-phone numbers. Let's keep in touch this time. If any of you are around the hotel at lunchtime, let's get together." The men agreed and Mike hurried outside to get a valet to bring his rental car.

Minutes later, he was striding toward Savannah Clay's office. He had dreamed unwanted dreams about her last night. Enticing dreams where she had been soft, willing and sexy in his arms. In real life, she was none of the above, he reminded himself. Instantly, he had to admit that his assessment was unfair. She probably was soft and sexy. Willing, on the other hand, with him never. When he opened the office door, the brunette receptionist flashed him a smile.

"Good morning, Colonel Remington. Miss Clay is expecting you. I'll tell her you're here, if you'll please be seated."

He sat in a brown, leather chair and moments later, the receptionist said, "Go on in. First door—"

"On the right," he finished, smiling at her. He reached the open door and was struck again by Savannah's beauty, restrained by her businesslike demeanor. She was standing in front of her desk, dressed in a tailored navy suit and navy blouse, her hair once again in a twist at the back of her head. But he remembered that cascade of silky, golden hair and the figure beneath the tailored suit jacket. Her skirt ended just above her knees, giving him a good view of her long legs.

She met his eyes and his pulse speeded up a notch. "Colonel Remington," she said politely, smiling at him. "Come in." She took his arm and wound it through hers, standing with their shoulders and hips touching, so close to him that he could feel her warmth. He could smell her perfume and was as dazzled by her as if he were fifteen years old again with a first crush.

Suddenly he became aware that they weren't the only people in the room. "Mike," she said, "I want you to meet Melanie Bradford, Jessie's caseworker."

He turned to shake hands with a brown-haired, fortyish woman, then stopped. The woman was holding a baby.

"And this is Jessie," Savannah announced, taking the baby and placing her swiftly in his arms.

Startled, he looked down at the baby he held so awkwardly. Big blue eyes gazed up at him as she pursed her rosebud mouth. She was soft, sweet-smelling and dressed in a frilly pink dress with a tiny pink hair bow in her wispy brown curls. She waved a fist at him.

"It's nice to meet you," Melanie Bradford said to him. "If you two will excuse me a moment, I need to call my office." When she left the room, Savannah closed the door behind her and leaned against it.

"This isn't going to make any difference," he said to Savannah.

"Will you just look at her? And think—over a million in cash in your account, a trust for you to raise her, which means a very generous income. Also, you get the house. Hire a nanny, for heaven's sake! You don't *have* to be tied down." Savannah's voice was low and seductive, trying to convince him.

When she walked over to him, he held out the baby for her to take.

"*You* hold her," Savannah insisted. "Look into her eyes and tell her that you're going to make her a ward of the state and let her be shuffled around to foster homes. Think of her dad and the trust and faith he placed in you." Now her voice held steel in it, and a good measure of anger, too.

"Stop trying to sell me on this, because it isn't going to work," Mike said tightly. "I'm *not* becoming guardian of a baby."

"Can you look at her and tell her that?"

He gazed down into wide blue eyes and remembered John Frates. "Dammit, leave me alone, Savannah. You don't push someone into parenthood," he said, his anger growing.

"Nonsense. Half the world gets pushed into it one way or another. Have you ever planned to marry, or do you plan to stay a bachelor your entire life?"

"I don't intend to get married yet," Mike replied in clipped tones.

"So you never expected to marry or have children."

"That isn't what I said," he snapped. "Now take this baby, Savannah. I'm afraid I'll drop her."

Jessie cooed, and as he watched, she smiled at him. He felt a tightening inside and a small sliver of regret. The girl caught his finger in her hand, holding it tightly.

He clenched his jaw and imagined life with a baby. He couldn't. He was headed for D.C. today and the CIA. They wouldn't like having a man saddled with a child. He couldn't settle in a little Texas town and take charge of a baby. Nor could he see taking her to Washington with him.

"She's beautiful," he said tersely, and held her out to Savannah again. "Thanks for giving me a lot of sleepless nights."

"I hope so," she answered in a voice dripping with disdain as she took Jessie and cuddled her in her arms. She crossed to the door, talking softly to the baby, looking as if she'd done this a million times before. She gave the baby to the caseworker and returned, closing the door and facing him. And once again, she took his breath away. How could the woman be so beautiful and so damned annoying at the same time?

"Will you at least go have coffee with me?" she asked. "I have one more thing I want to show you."

"One more reason to ruin my life?"

"If you have a guilty conscience, that's not my fault," she replied with a smugness that only heightened his irritation.

"Yeah, sure," he said. "I'll go, but I don't see any point in us spending one more minute together."

"I think another couple of hours is a small thing to ask. Are you this difficult with other women?"

"This isn't a man-woman thing and you know it."

She gave him a long, intense look that included a sweep of her eyes from his head to his toes and back, and he had to admit to himself that it was at least partially a man-woman thing.

"No, I guess it's not," she said coolly, making him want to cross the room and take her in his arms, kiss her soundly and show her it was a man-woman thing after all. "But I'd really like you to spend the next couple of hours with me." She awarded him the dazzling smile that made his knees weak, and he wondered how many juries and judges had succumbed to the influence of that smile.

"What the hey," he said, and grinned. "I have hours yet to kill here." He strolled over to her and she gazed up at him, the smile still hovering on her lips. If his proximity fazed her, she didn't show it. "Maybe it could turn into a man-woman thing," he said softly.

"Not in this lifetime," she snapped. "But I'm glad you've agreed to stay. Let me arrange a few things, and then we're out of here. Wait just a minute."

Another order. Did the woman even know the word *please?* he wondered. He sat and watched her move around her office, and in minutes she nodded to him. "I'm ready. Shall we go?"

He left with her, enjoying the sight of her walking beside him, as well as the scent of her perfume. "Is this another exercise in futility?" he asked.

"Might be, but I have to do what I have to do. I don't give up easily."

"You're very passionate about this. Maybe all that passion is just misguided."

She laughed, a sexy, flirty laugh, then slanted him a look that made his blood heat. "In your dreams, Colonel! You're not goading me into sex."

"Sometimes the impossible happens," he retorted lightly, but she was definitely keeping him off balance. He didn't want to be intrigued by her or physically drawn to her, but he was. A woman who kept shifting from glacial to this kind of sexy was bound to give him trouble.

At her car he held the door for her and then went around to sit in the passenger seat. As they drove away from her office and into San Antonio traffic, he watched her.

When they left town and traffic thinned, his curiosity increased. He looked at rolling green hills dotted with sturdy oaks and sprinkled with colorful wildflowers. "So where are we headed—Stallion Pass, perhaps?"

"Good guess. I want you to see the town."

"It won't do you any good."

"You asked me last night, and now I'll ask you—have you ever been in love?"

"Yes, I have," he answered quickly.

"I'll bet lots of times," she said, flashing a quick smile.

"Sometimes it's a light, pleasure-only thing and sometimes it's been more serious, but nothing permanent ever. I'm not a man to settle, and women take a dim view of getting involved with a man with my lifestyle."

"Why do I doubt that they protest very much? I'll bet you're nearly always the one to break things off."

"Why would you think that?"

"You're handsome, dynamic, aggressive—"

"Aggressive? I think I've been a model of restraint and cooperation with one exception. I'm *not* taking a baby as an inheritance."

"You might change your mind."

"No, I won't. Handsome?" he repeated, his tone changing as he shifted slightly in the seat to study her more intently. "My, my, Counselor. I'm surprised to get any kind of positive reaction from you," he said.

"You didn't, but I imagine ninety-five percent of the women you meet find you quite attractive."

"Now what exactly makes you come to that conclusion?"

She laughed and glanced at him. "You want me to shower you with compliments? I think your ego is big enough as it is."

"And I bet you get hit on often, too. Except you probably scare the hell out of a lot of men."

"Do I scare *you?*" she asked, slanting him another quick, saucy look.

"Ask me that when you're not driving, and I'll show you."

"Why do you want to be in the CIA?"

"You're changing the subject, but I'll remind you of it later," Mike told her. "I want to go into the CIA because I can still serve my country that way. I can do some interesting things, see interesting places."

"You can do that in the military, too. Why are you getting out?"

"It's a little too much on the edge. I'm tired of getting shot at."

"And that won't happen in the CIA?"

"I'm wrangling for a desk job."

"I'm surprised," she said. "You look the type for action."

"What kind of lawyer are you? Estate planning?"

"Contract law is my specialty, but I do estates. I've done a lot of work for John Frates because we've known each other all our lives."

"You're a lot younger than John Frates."

She smiled at him. "Thanks, but you don't know how old I am."

"I'd guess twenty-eight," Mike said, his gaze drifting up and down her.

"Guessing a woman's age is a risky business. I'm thirty."

"Ten years younger than John."

"You remember his age?" She shot Mike a surprised glance.

"I had to know a lot about John before we went to get him. Personal information helps."

As she smiled at him, Mike suspected she knew a lot about his background. They talked while they drove through small towns and across the Texas countryside until finally they reached the outskirts of a town, where a rock wall held a sign that read Welcome to Stallion Pass.

"So where's the pass?"

"There isn't one. It goes back to an early-day legend of an Apache warrior who fell in love with a cavalryman's daughter. The soldiers killed the warrior, and according to legend, his ghost was a wild, white stallion that forever roamed these parts looking for his true love. According to the legend, whoever caught the stallion would find love. Anyway, the town got the name Stallion Pass because there have been wild, white stallions around these parts forever."

"Is there one now?"

"The last one I heard about was fairly recent. One of the ranchers here caught a white stallion. He passed it on to one of his friends, who gave it to another friend."

"And did love come to them?"

She smiled. "All of those guys are married now—you be the judge."

Mike smiled back at her. "You can be charming when you want to be."

"So can you, Mike. Truce?"

"Until we talk about babies and settling in small towns."

She wrinkled her nose but didn't challenge him. "Now we're coming into the central part of Stallion Pass. This town was established right after the Civil War because there was an early fort outside of town. Then the railroad came through here and the town boomed. The Frateses were one of the early families. So were the Clays. Most people have stayed. There's a lot of oil money here, lots of ranches in the area, a refinery, some small industry in Stallion Pass, so we have a prosperous town. There's a museum, a civic center, a fine aquarium and botanical gardens."

She pointed out sights to him while he looked at two new hotels a block from an older, renovated one. "That's the Wentworth Hotel, one of the oldest in Texas, although not as old as the Menger in San Antonio. Across the street is the best steak house in these parts, Murphy's Steakhouse.

It's excellent. A few blocks over is an equally good restaurant—only, barbecue is the specialty.''

He looked at sights she pointed out, realizing that ''prosperous'' was an understatement. The town looked like the product of both old and new money, with its fancy shops, restaurants and office buildings surrounding a green, tree-shaded town square with a large, three-tiered fountain gushing sparkling water.

The houses around town were old and well-kept, but as he and Savannah drove out of town, the houses changed to newer structures. Soon Savannah turned between iron gates into an area of enormous mansions.

He saw a sign that read Woodbridge and gazed beyond it at sprawling, well-tended lawns and multicolored flowerbeds.

''Looks like there's a lot of money in this little town,'' Mike said, looking at a mansion set back from the road, a winding, tree-lined drive leading up to the front door. ''It's not going to do you any good to show me the house I can inherit,'' he said quietly. ''This isn't my style.''

''What *is* your style, Mike?''

''Small apartments, my books, my bike. I don't have a lot of possessions. I've lived on military bases and moved around a lot.''

''The house comes furnished,'' she said as she turned up the long, winding drive.

''That won't matter,'' he replied. Mike looked at the three-story, redbrick Georgian. White columns supported the roof of a wide front porch.

''This is the Frateses' home, which you have now inherited.'' She stopped and turned off the engine.

He caught her wrist, instantly more aware of the physical contact than what he was about to tell her. ''This is a waste of time. I was never meant for a house like this. I've never even dreamed of a house like this.''

''So sell it and get something you like. Right now, it's

yours, so let's go look at it. C'mon.'' She twisted her wrist out of his light grasp and climbed out.

Mike got out, too, and walked around, truly not interested in the house and unable to relate to it in any manner.

He stood in the enormous front hallway and looked at the crystal chandelier overhead, the winding staircase and the elegant furnishings. She caught his hand. ''Come with me.''

Once again, the moment she touched him, he was focused completely on her. He went upstairs with her and knew where she was taking him before they entered a little girl's bedroom filled with toys, pink ruffles and fancy white furniture.

''I figured this was where we were going,'' he said when she stopped in the middle of the room and dropped his hand.

''This is what you're taking her away from.''

''You're a smart lawyer. I'm sure you can work out something.''

''While I work out something, she'll belong to the state. Those bureaucratic things take lots of time and red tape.''

''So you told me,'' he said. ''The answer is still no.''

She turned to stare at him. ''I think you're being incredibly selfish. You could take Jessie and have all this! Hire a staff to care for her.''

''If I took her, I couldn't live with that,'' he said quietly, wanting to leave.

''Instead, you'll give her up to strangers,'' Savannah said, fire flashing in the depths of her eyes.

Mike felt his own temper rise. ''Why don't you take her? You're so all-fired eager to get Jessie someone who cares. Though I am surprised you care. You're—'' He broke off.

''What?'' she asked, looking amused. ''Hard?''

He gazed into her eyes and shook his head. ''Tough, but never hard. There isn't a hard part in you. You're delectably soft,'' he said quietly, watching her blink and realizing for once he had caught her so by surprise that she hadn't been able to hide it. "Maybe you're stubborn and aggressive, but definitely soft."

"Me, stubborn? *You* take the prize."

"I'll tell you one thing I am," he said in the same quiet voice, aware of her as a woman, inhaling her perfume, standing only a few feet from her. "I'm curious. Before I get on that plane to D.C., I'd like to satisfy my curiosity." He moved closer and slid his hand behind her head.

He expected her to step back and snap at him, but when she didn't, he looked into her eyes and saw she wasn't going to say no. He saw the same curiosity *he* had.

He leaned the last bit of distance and brushed her lips with his, and then his mouth settled on hers. Her mouth was a warm, soft invitation, her lips parting and her sweet breath rushing out.

The moment his tongue touched hers, he felt a jolt. He slipped his arm around her waist and pulled her to him, and discovered he had been right. She was all soft curves.

To his surprise, as he kissed her, the sparks that danced in the air so often between them turned to flames. She set him ablaze with her kiss as their tongues played together. Her kiss became more than he had expected. He was shaken to his toes and on fire, a searing heat making him tight and hard. He pulled her closer, dimly aware her hands were on his upper arms.

She aroused him, and he wanted her to an extent that surprised him. He was caught in a kiss that put fire in his veins. His heart pounded and his blood roared, and her kiss turned out to be more than he'd ever dreamed possible. The magnitude of his desire was startling. He wanted to take down her hair, push off the suit jacket; he wanted to peel away all their clothes, get rid of the bothersome barriers between them.

When she pushed against his chest, he released her. "I'll cancel my plane if you'll go to dinner with me tonight," he said in a husky voice, wanting to pull her back into his arms.

He felt as if he had opened Pandora's box and trouble was spilling out all around him. A part of him didn't want to cancel his plane reservation and spend hours with her. Another part of him didn't want to let her out of his sight. "And not one word about babies."

The fires in the depth of her blue eyes became frost.

"You get on your plane and go on with your self-centered life," she snapped.

Maybe passion pushed his temper to an edge, but he was tired of her calling him selfish and self-centered. "I've said it before and I'll say it again. Why don't *you* take her?"

"I might try to gain custody of her, but it still means up to two years of shuffling little Jessie through the system. And there's no guarantee I'd get her."

"If you've known John all your life, I don't know why you didn't inherit her in the first place."

She flinched and drew a deep breath. "I've wondered why he didn't ask me, too, because I gladly would have taken Jessie," Savannah replied stiffly. "I've known John forever. Maybe that's one reason I've been so in your face about this. I wish it had been me—not for the money or house, but for Jessie. I think she's adorable."

"Yeah, right," he said, thinking that Savannah put on a good act.

She bristled. "You don't believe me?"

"It's easy to say you'd take her when you know you can't. And I don't think you'll fight to get her, either. The situation looks different when you're the one who has to take the lifetime responsibility."

"That's not so!" Savannah's cheeks flushed angrily. "If I had the chance, I'd take her in a second."

"Right," he replied in a voice dripping with sarcasm. He tilted his head to study her. "Hell, marry me—a marriage of convenience—and then you can take her."

"Marry you! That would be like putting a lion and a tiger in a cage together."

"Yeah, exactly. Marry me," he said, glad to put her on the defensive. "I'll stay as long as necessary, and then you can have the care of her and go through all the red tape to legally get custody."

"Don't be ridiculous," she said, her voice laced with disgust.

Satisfied that he had proved his point, he put his hands on his hips. "You're not jumping at this chance to give little Jessie a family and a home? I didn't think you would. When the shoe's on the other foot, it's mighty different. Now you don't want any part of it."

"That isn't because of Jessie."

"You and I could stay in this mansion and never see each other," he argued, glad to keep her on the defensive. "It's huge."

"Nothing is *that* huge."

"Yeah, right, Counselor. You just don't want the responsibility. Now we could argue all day, but I've got a plane to catch."

He left the room. Savannah glared at him and wanted to shake her fist and scream. Insufferable man! She didn't want to think about his devastating kiss. Life wasn't fair. He was so cussed stubborn and unrelenting. She didn't want to dream about him after he had flown out of her life this afternoon. And she didn't want to cry over Jessie and remember cold, frightened nights in her own life.

Jessie's a baby, too little right now to be scared or know what was happening to her, Savannah thought sternly, then instantly rejected that notion.

She hurried after Mike, looking at his squared shoulders and long, forceful stride. He acted as though he ruled the world.

He didn't believe she would take Jessie if she had the chance, but she would. He saw her as a tough lawyer who was all business, but she would love to have Jessie. It had hurt that John hadn't asked her to be Jessie's guardian.

Apart from their families having been close, John's business had helped make her and Troy's practice a big success. At the time she read the will, she had thought he was as close as a brother to Mike Remington, and that was why he wanted Mike to be Jessie's guardian. Since meeting Mike, she realized he couldn't have really known Mike or foreseen that Mike would refuse.

Now this infuriating man who made her grit her teeth, who could kiss a woman into a pool of quivering jelly, was going to walk out and leave the baby to become a ward of the state.

Marry him! That certainly *would* be like putting a lion and a tiger into a cage together. And he hadn't really meant it, anyway. Marriage would tie him down more than simply taking Jessie and hiring nannies. Unless he thought he could get a wife and vanish for months at a time.

She didn't know what was in that handsome head of his. She glared at him as he went through the front door while she followed and locked up.

When she turned, he held out his hand. "Give me the keys and I'll drive. It'll give you a break."

"I'm not trusting you with my car," she said tersely, annoyed with him, wanting to shake him and hating that she was too cognizant of his appeal. For if she reached out to shake him, the touch would ignite the volatile chemistry between them.

She thought about the dinner date she had turned down. More kisses—the thought of more of his kisses sent her pulse into a dizzying spiral. Yet the evening would be another exercise in futility, getting her all hot and bothered in every way.

A marriage of convenience to Mike Remington. It would be war. Even if he had meant it, she couldn't tie her life to his, not even as a technicality.

When he held the door for her, she was acutely conscious of passing close to him, of his dark eyes steadily watching her. The man was incredibly sexy, and her nerves were jangled because of him.

She slid behind the wheel and glanced up to catch him looking at her legs. His gaze met hers, and then he closed the door and strode around the front of the car to get into the passenger side.

"Friends, Counselor?" he asked as she turned down the long driveway.

"Hardly," she answered coolly, wondering if he had been affected at all by their kiss. Maybe a little, since he had offered to cancel his flight and take her to dinner.

After a silent ride, as they stood in the parking lot at her office, they faced each other and he held out his hand. "It's been interesting. I'm sorry, but I can't become guardian of a baby. I'm sure you'll find someone who can take Jessie. You gave it a real good try."

"Don't patronize me," she said, annoyed with him, yet far too responsive to him, tingling because of his hand holding hers and mesmerized by his midnight-brown eyes, which held dark temptations and secrets. Sexy eyes that made her pulse race when he gave her one of his steady, probing looks. "I'll be back in touch with you," she said. "It isn't often someone turns down a million-dollar inheritance. I don't know the precedents."

"Take your time, Counselor. You have my number in D.C. It's been interesting."

"Have a nice life," she snapped, turning to walk away and wondering how long it would take her to get over her anger toward him. And how long would it take her to forget his sexy kiss?

Mike drove out of the shaded lot, glancing in the rearview mirror to see Savannah standing at the door watching him drive away. Stubborn woman. But, oh, so sexy. What a kiss!

He was going home to Washington, and he was certain Savannah would find a guardian for Jessie.

Forgetting Stallion Pass, Jessie and Savannah Clay, Mike

turned his thoughts to D.C. and the appointments he had, things he had to do.

At the airport, he milled with the crowd until his plane was called. Picking up his carry-on and a newspaper, he lined up as the first people moved into the jetway.

"Mike!"

"Would Mike Remington please come to the desk," came an announcement over the intercom. He turned, first to see who had called his name.

"Mike!"

Surprised, he saw Savannah hurrying toward him. "Mike, wait!" she called and waved.

The first thought that came to mind was that he had forgotten something, but he had brought hardly anything with him and he was certain he hadn't left any possession with Savannah.

"Mike, wait!" she cried, getting closer. "I'll marry you."

Three

Mike was certain he hadn't heard correctly. He stared at her as she came rushing up to him.

"I'll marry you!" she cried again as she stopped only a few feet from him.

"You're crazy," he said, staring at her in dismay.

"Would Mike Remington please report to the desk?" a voice said over the intercom.

"Go tell them to cancel that announcement," she said breathlessly, staring at him.

Transfixed, he could only stare back. "You were right earlier. You and I can't marry," he said, never for one second thinking she would take him up on his offhand suggestion that they have a marriage of convenience.

"I thought about it," she said, and he was only dimly aware of people moving around them. They had suddenly been shut off from the rest of the world. The moment was surreal; the concept of any kind of long-lasting contract with her was an absolute impossibility. But she was standing there in front of him, still in her tailored navy suit and blouse, a couple of loose, golden tendrils curling around her face, and she looked and sounded earnest.

"Would Mike Remington please report to the desk."

"Just a minute," he said to Savannah. "Let me get them to stop paging me."

"They're paging you because I asked them to. I was afraid you'd already be on your plane."

He nodded and rushed to the desk to tell them the person who had been looking for him had found him. He also canceled his flight. When he turned away from the counter, he saw Savannah standing to one side of the hall, waiting for him solemnly. She looked pale and uncertain, something else he wouldn't have expected.

He crossed to her and took her arm. "Let's go where we can talk."

In minutes they were in a quiet, deserted airport bar. He had ordered a soda for her and beer for him. Stunned, he still couldn't accept the past few minutes.

He sat facing her. "I can't believe that you'd marry me. And frankly, I didn't give the offer much thought."

"I figured you'd try to wriggle out of it."

"Not necessarily. I'm just surprised. What made you change your mind?"

"I've thought about this—not marriage, but what to do about Jessie. If we have a marriage of convenience, I'd get Jessie right now. You'd be the official guardian, but you can do as you damn well please. You'll be an instant millionaire. I have enough money to take care of my needs and Jessie's, although there is a trust for that and a trust for her."

"You said it yourself—it would be like putting a lion and a tiger together," he reminded her, appalled that she had taken him up on such an impossible offer.

"So you didn't mean it and you're weaseling out?" she asked, sparks flying in her eyes again.

His anger flared, and he took a deep breath, hanging on to his temper. "I'm not weaseling out, but I don't think it's a smart move."

"What else will keep Jessie from becoming a ward of the state?"

They glared at each other as he took a long swallow of beer. He wanted to shake her and he wanted to walk away. Tell her no and grab the next flight and get out of Texas. On the other hand, she had a point. He could do as he pleased, leave the baby with her, and Jessie wouldn't be turned over to the state. That should make them both happy. And getting the chance to see Savannah soft and warm again was very appealing.

"Could you adopt her if we were married?" he asked her.

"I think we would have to do it as man and wife, then we could get a divorce. Otherwise, you're her legal guardian and it would be complicated if not impossible. I'll look into it. We adopt, and then we could break up the marriage and you would be free. Surely that isn't asking too much of you to give."

"Listen, Savannah, I'm tired of you painting me as the bad guy just because I don't want this responsibility. This was thrust on me without my knowledge or consent."

"Sorry," she said.

"You don't mean that," he accused, thinking about what she had said. "Before we rush out and say vows, let's sleep on this tonight."

"That's fine with me," she answered, suddenly bestowing one of those win-over-the-world smiles on him. "Why don't you let me cook dinner for you? Come to my place about seven o'clock."

"I have to get a hotel room and a car...."

"You could stay at my place," she told him a bit desperately.

"Thanks, Savannah. Your place will be great tonight since I might have trouble getting a room this late," he said, wanting to mess up her day as much as she had ruined his. "This will give us a chance to see if we can tolerate being under the same roof together."

She flashed another knee-melting smile at him. "You surprise me again, Mike. But remember, my condo is far smaller than that Stallion Pass mansion. At my place we'll *know* we're together."

"Now who's trying to weasel out of an invitation?"

"Not on your life," she said, reaching over to give his arm a squeeze. "I'm delighted. Let's go."

"All right," he answered, amused that she was taking charge and making decisions again, mindful of the current that ripped through him when she touched his arm.

They left, and in minutes were headed into the heart of the city. At her condo, she opened the door and led him inside. "I'll put steaks out to grill—how's that?"

"Sounds fine, Savannah," he replied, looking around at oak cabinets and woodwork, green plants, a yellow-tile counter, a glass-top table, expensive furnishings and state-of-the-art kitchen equipment.

"Come with me and I'll show you around," she said, leading him into a large living area with a stone fireplace, a big-screen television, a polished hardwood floor and elegant fruitwood furniture. "Here's where I spend most of my time. There's the dining room," she said with a wave of her hand. Through an open doorway, he saw a crystal chandelier hanging above a long, oval wooden table and chairs. "Your room is this way."

"This is very nice," Mike remarked as he walked beside her.

"Thank you. I like it, but my favorite place is my home

in Stallion Pass. It's near one of my brothers and his family, and one of my sisters and her family. There's my office," she said, waving her hand at another open door. He saw a neat desk with a computer and printer, bookshelves filled with law books.

"You can stay in here," she said, entering a room on her right that had green-and-beige decor, a four-poster bed, mahogany furniture and a hardwood floor. "There's an adjoining bathroom and clean towels are already set out. Anything you need, you can let me know."

He turned to face her, meeting her wide, blue eyes. "And where will *you* be?"

"My room is right down the hall," she replied.

"Don't you think you're rushing into this? You don't look like the impetuous type. No lawyer does."

"You're making more snap judgments," she said. "I'm not given to acting impulsively on whims, but time was running out on this one. I suspected that if you got on that plane to D.C., I'd have a difficult time getting you back to Texas."

"You figured that one right, but I think we both ought to give this marriage idea more thought."

She smiled. "Marriage, even a paper one, scares you, doesn't it?"

"Damn straight!" he snapped. "I'll be signing a contract and agreeing to certain things that will change my life. I have to give this more thought."

"Even though you proposed it. You didn't expect me to take you up on it, did you."

As he looked into her big, blue eyes, he again felt the clash of wills, along with sparks. He couldn't keep from smiling and shrugging. "You got me on that one."

"You're here to give it some more thought. In the meantime, let me freshen up and change into something comfortable, and I'll see you in the kitchen in about half an hour.'' Her eyes sparkled, and he knew he was sinking in quicksand.

"Sure." He watched her walk away, an easy thing to do. She had a nice walk, but the suit jacket hid a lot. He was glad she was changing into something else.

He followed her and stood in the doorway, watching her turn into another room down the hall and close the door behind her. He closed his door and glanced at his watch. He had calls to make to people in D.C., plans to change. Now when would he go home? Probably tomorrow, whatever they decided.

Marry Savannah Clay. The thought was staggering. He'd come to Texas thinking he would get a small inheritance, see old friends and then return to his life. Instead, here he was in the home of a woman he'd known less than twenty-four hours, contemplating becoming her husband and the guardian of another man's baby. Talk about being sucker-punched, he thought—and he'd helped Savannah deliver this blow.

A marriage of convenience to Savannah, even if they were in that mansion and if the marriage was a paper one and if the union only lasted briefly. Could he do it? She was aggressive, stubborn, accustomed to getting her way, outspoken. And sexy. Suppose that got mixed up in the equation? No danger of falling in love, though. Maybe they were too much alike. Both of them were strong-willed people with explosive tempers.

He showered and changed into jeans and a blue knit shirt, pulling on clean socks and loafers. His thoughts churned with the possibilities and hazards before him. He never for an instant thought she would take him up on his offer of a paper marriage. He was still astounded that she had, yet he could certainly see how it would get her what she wanted.

He guessed he could do it and still go on with his life. Before starting a new job, he had intended to take a month off, anyway. He wanted some rest and relaxation. He wouldn't get that with Savannah and a baby, but he could escape most of the time and still enjoy a vacation.

He thought of John Frates, a nice enough person but not one Mike had been unusually close to. As Mike combed his hair, he sighed. He didn't want to stay in Texas and embark on a marriage of convenience, but it would give Savannah what she wanted, it would give the baby a real home, and there really wasn't any good reason for him not to consent to it. Not when he looked at it logically. Especially since he'd practically dared Savannah to take him up on it. But when he considered the plan with his heart, he didn't want any part of it.

Go on, Remington, he told himself. Make them happy, then get out of Texas and on with your life. He glanced at his watch, sighed and left to find Savannah.

She was nowhere around, so he went out on the patio and sat on a comfortable padded chair, enjoying the shade and breeze until he heard the door behind him slide open as Savannah stepped outside. He came to his feet and turned to her.

She wore a red T-shirt, denim cutoffs and sandals. Her hair was in a long braid, and for a moment he was transfixed, staring at her. She looked about seventeen. Which was interesting because he suddenly felt about seventeen. Her figure was amazing, her bare, long legs fabulous.

"Wow, Counselor, you clean up good," he said appreciatively, momentarily forgetting the problem, unable to keep from looking at her from head to toe while she smiled at him.

"Thanks. Can I get you something to drink?"

"Sure. Got any cold beer?"

"Yes, I do."

He trailed after her and watched her move around the kitchen, bending down to get their drinks from the fridge, which gave him an enticing look at her trim derriere and let his imagination run wild. She handed him a beer and got a bottle of pop for herself. When she got out steaks, he took the platter from her, their hands brushing.

"I'll cook these," he said, then carrying them out to the patio, where he fired up the barbecue and minutes later put them on. He returned to the kitchen to watch her as she tossed a green salad.

"What's the real reason, Savannah, that you want to take the responsibility for a baby?" he asked quietly. She was making an enormous sacrifice to bring the baby into her life, and he wondered if there was more to her motives than she was telling him. When she gave him a wide-eyed look, studying him in silence before she looked away and went back to the salad, he was certain he had guessed correctly.

"I've told you that I can't bear to see her become a ward of the state," she said. "Remember, I'd known John Frates forever. He was like one of my brothers," she said carefully, and Mike caught an undercurrent of tension.

Mike set down his beer and moved closer, tilting up her chin and looking intently at her. "I think it's more than that," he said.

She inhaled swiftly and jerked her chin away. Then she peeled a tomato swiftly and chopped it.

"Most of the time I can hide my feelings pretty well. No one gets what I truly think or feel. I'm surprised you're the person who has managed to do that. Maybe when I know you better, I'll tell you, because it's a long story," she said without looking up at him.

So the lady lawyer was hiding something from her past that made her want to take care of this little baby. "Why on earth didn't John pick your brother to take Jessie?"

"My brothers all have kids now and he may have thought they wouldn't want another one. I don't know. I can't figure it." She paused and cast him a look. "I don't know what he saw in you—or the other guys, for that matter. He had close friends here. He didn't have relatives, but none of you were that close to him.''

''I told you before,'' Mike said, leaning back against the counter and crossing his feet at the ankle, ''people develop strong feelings for those who save them from an intolerable, life-threatening situation. They tortured him and he was in bad shape. He was grateful, but his will was a real surprise to all of us.''

''I'm thirty now,'' Savannah said, moving around the kitchen. ''I don't know that I'll ever marry. I'd like a baby, and Jessie needs someone, so it seems like a logical answer for both our problems.''

''Thirty isn't exactly over the hill.''

''No, but I've got my career, and as you said, I probably scare some men. I know I'm a little aggressive, but I have to be in my line of work.''

''So you admit it,'' he said, watching while she finished the salad, put two potatoes in the microwave, then got out bread and butter.

''Yes. Will you admit it about yourself?'' she asked, pausing to look him in the eye.

He shrugged. ''I sure as hell have had to be aggressive in my job.''

''I guess that's why we clash so much. We're both accustomed to getting our way.''

''Or at least trying to,'' he said. ''I don't always.''

''When haven't you?''

''When I haven't saved someone,'' he said, setting his beer on the counter. ''I'll check on the steaks.''

''We'll eat outside. Here, you can set the table,'' she said, handing him plates, silverware and napkins. He was aware that their hands brushed again. He felt too conscious of her now that she was in cutoffs and the tight T-shirt.

Later, when they sat down to dinner on the patio and had

cut into thick, juicy steaks, she asked him, "So who have you lost or failed to save?"

"One hostage, several buddies."

"You don't want to talk about it."

"Not really," he answered, remembering Colin Garrick. Colin should be here in Texas with the rest of them. The memory still hurt. Colin had been with them when they rescued John Frates. But then the next year in Makeyevka, Colin had been killed when they had been on a covert assignment to rescue a CIA agent being held hostage. Mike hadn't been able to save Colin. Mike's jaw clamped. It hurt to remember, and it was one of the reasons he was getting out of the service. He had lost Colin, his best buddy. He'd known the man since he was just a kid. Then there were Dusty and Jack. All good guys. All needless, senseless deaths in the line of duty. Mike tried to shut his mind to the bad memories as he cut into the steak.

"So what do you think now about this marriage you proposed?" she asked.

"I'm thinking about it," he replied, watching her cut her steak. She had long, slender fingers, tapered nails and delicate wrists. "I'll admit I don't want to do it, but at the same time, it might work. I want a prenuptial agreement."

"And you think I don't?"

"As far as I'm concerned, Savannah, I don't want John Frates's money. If you get Jessie, you can keep it for her or for yourself, or give it to charity."

"I don't run across many people who would turn down over a million-dollar inheritance or offer to give the money away," she said, sounding puzzled while curiosity filled her eyes. "Why would you do that?"

He shrugged. "I lead a simple life. I have simple needs. Sure, I like money. I have saved money and invested money. I want to retire when I'm young enough to enjoy life, but I don't want a mansion or a lot of things. My folks didn't have it real easy some years when I was growing up, and I know how to do without. I don't have a lot of possessions. Money's not a big deal in my life. Is it in yours?''

''I'll admit I want security and comfort.''

''You've got that already, I'd say,'' he said, looking through the open back door at a kitchen elegant enough to be in a decorator magazine.

''Your family is scattered,'' she said. ''Do you ever see them?''

''Usually we get together at Christmas or other holidays. What about your family?''

''My entire family lives in this area, so we see each other a lot. My folks live out of town a short way and have horses, and we all get together to ride once or twice a month.''

''You said you have brothers and sisters, right?'' he asked as he cut into his steak again.

I have three brothers. Two of them, Andy and Jacob, work with my dad in his insurance business.''

''What does your other brother do?''

''Lucius, my oldest brother, is a ranch foreman south of here. All the rest of my siblings live in Stallion Pass. I have twelve nieces and nephews, so there's always a lot of children around.''

''Wow, big family. What about your partner?'' he asked, still feeling she was holding back her true reason for battling him to take Jessie. ''He's single. I'm surprised the two of you aren't dating.''

''How do you know he's single?''

''He wasn't wearing a wedding ring.''

''You're observant,'' she said.

Mike shrugged. ''It goes with my job.''

''We did date briefly, but I broke it off. He's not the man for me. We're just good friends now.''

Mike finished his dinner and sipped his water, watching

her take dainty bites. He'd like to reach over and undo that braid, let her hair loose the way it had been last night.

They finished dinner with scoops of strawberry ice cream. When they carried their dishes back to the kitchen to clean, Mike was aware of moving around her, occasionally brushing against her or touching hands as they passed each other dishes. As soon as they finished clearing the table, they returned to sit on the patio. The sun had slipped below the horizon and dusk had set in. There was a cool breeze, and when she sat down, Mike pulled his chair closer to hers, sitting so he could face her. He wanted to look at her.

Savannah was very aware of him. It had been a long time since a man had been in her condo. None had ever slept here, and Mike's presence was disturbing. She was more on edge than in the fiercest trial she'd ever had to deal with. It was an enormous decision to take him up on his offer of marriage, albeit a paper one only.

His reluctance didn't help her feelings about the decision. How was she ever going to break the news to her family? She didn't want a sham marriage to a man she clashed with constantly, yet it would mean getting Jessie. In some ways Savannah barely knew Mike, and in others she felt as if she had known him a long time because she had listened to John talk about each one of the men, Mike in particular.

How could John have been so convinced of Mike's friendship and goodness and been so abysmally wrong?

"I'll have to admit," Mike said, "I have butterflies about this, but it seems like the only answer."

They looked at each other in silence, and he saw as much uncertainty and distaste in her eyes as he was experiencing, but another undercurrent sizzled in him, an intense awareness of her as a beautiful, desirable woman. He wanted her, and if their lives were going to be united, he might just get her.

Something flickered in the depths of her eyes and she

looked down, breaking eye contact. When she glanced up again, she said, "We need to work out a few details. Under the circumstances, any kind of formal wedding would be absurd."

He arched a brow. "You don't think you'll ever marry. If you want this to be your fancy wedding, I can handle that. I don't think the groom is usually all that involved, anyway."

"With my family you'd be involved," she said, kicking off her sneakers and folding her legs under her. "They're going to see through this marriage instantly, so we might as well be up-front with them. The trouble is, I come from a big family and we've lived in Stallion Pass forever and been involved with people in San Antonio. There will be worlds of friends to notify. I can't get married and just tell people when I see them."

"Looks to me like you've come right back to a big wedding."

She bit her lip and stared beyond him.

He moved his chair near hers. "Stay where you are," he said quietly when she started to turn. "I want to fix something."

Savannah felt his hands moving and realized he was unbraiding her hair. She glanced over her shoulder at him. "Why are you doing that?" she asked in amusement.

"I like you best with your hair down and loose. It's too pretty for this braid."

"I wasn't sure you approved of much of anything about me."

"You know better than that," he said softly. "I approved of your kiss enough to offer to cancel my flight and take you to dinner tonight—which we kind of ended up doing, anyway. I approve of your looks, your long legs, the way your skin feels," he said quietly, and brushed a kiss across her nape.

She wondered if her pounding pulse was going to drown out his words. His breath was warm, his lips made her tingle and want to turn into his arms, which she did. When she looked into his eyes, she lost her breath. Then his mouth covered hers and his arm slipped around her waist. He turned her while he leaned over her and kissed her thoroughly.

Her insides were jelly, her desire a hot flame that licked through her veins. She slid her hands along his upper arms, feeling his solid muscles. As she wrapped her arms around his neck, she knew dimly that she was on dangerous ground. This was not a man to take lightly and not a man with whom to involve her heart. He had made it clear that eventually he was going to vanish from her life.

But at the moment she was lost in his kisses. Thought spun away and her need escalated. Passion blazed between them, and he shifted his chair and pulled her across his lap, cradling her head against his shoulder while he kissed her.

His hard shaft pressed against her hip, and she knew she had to stop him. Yet she badly wanted more of his kisses, more of him....

She put her hands against his muscled chest. "Mike," she whispered, tearing her lips from his, wanting to hold him, not push him away. "Mike, you're going far too fast."

He looked down at her, and the desire that blazed in his dark gaze made her heart thud. He relaxed his hold and she slipped off his lap, moving back to her chair. She felt completely off balance, something she rarely was.

"We're going to marry—" he began.

"In name only," she interrupted him. "*Absolutely* in name only. Don't ever expect anything else!"

"Scared, Counselor? Scared to let go and live a little?" he asked, amusement in his voice. "Don't worry, I know it won't be a real marriage. It's a temporary fix and then I'll go on with my life, but in the meantime, kisses are something both of us like and want.''

"Kisses are dangerous. I know you'll never have your heart in this marriage and you'll walk out of it all too soon."

He nodded. "You're right. I don't exactly think your heart will be in it, either. That tiger-and-lion thing."

"But maybe we can get along."

"I know one place we can get along," he said. "We've never had a real date. All this baby business is hanging between us."

"It isn't going away, and tonight is as real a date as we're ever going to have. Now let's plan the marriage, and I'll draw up a prenup agreement—but I'm not taking the money that John wanted to be yours."

"Split it then. Take half."

"What about the house?"

"It's yours."

"I don't really understand how you can so easily let go of such a marvelous inheritance."

"I guess I've lived on an edge where each day you're thankful to be alive. Life itself is a fabulous gift. I've seen so much ugly, senseless death and war and hatred that material things have little importance."

In that moment, she thought perhaps she glimpsed a little of the Mike that John Frates knew. "That's a sobering way of looking at everything."

"You get the house, half the money. The trusts are already set, aren't they?"

"Yes, they are. Maybe if we elope, come back, let my family throw a big party to announce our marriage—that might be the simplest way."

"Can you elope and not have your family there for your wedding? Even if it isn't exactly real?" he asked, reaching out to rest his arm on her shoulder while his hand played with her hair.

She felt every tiny tug against her scalp, and it made her unable to concentrate fully on the conversation.

She bit her lip and stared beyond him. He waited in silence. Savannah could tell her family the truth of the situation, but they would still want to be there, and they were all going to love little Jessie. She shifted her gaze to Mike to find him watching her. "You're right. My family will want to be there. And truthfully, I want them to be there. So now, do we have a small wedding and they throw a party for us afterward or a big wedding and get it over with?"

"It's your call on this one. I'll be present at whichever one you choose," he said.

"You have your moments when you're surprisingly cooperative," she said while half of her attention was on his fingers still tangled in her hair.

"Don't sound so shocked," he said.

She thought about what she wanted and what her family would like. "I guess I'll go for the big wedding."

"I think you're wrong about never marrying," he said quietly, leaning closer to tuck her hair behind her ear. The light brushing of his fingers against her increased the tingles she felt. Why did he have this intense effect on her, one that guys she'd dated hadn't had?

"Maybe, but I'm getting older and I don't see any looming prospects," she answered lightly, realizing there was more here than she had bargained for. Mike was sexy, far too appealing, and he liked to flirt. He probably flirted as automatically as breathing. "Let me call my folks and take you out there to meet them."

"Sure," he said, amused and knowing that she would take charge of everything from this point on. All he would have to do was put in appearances at the appointed times. "I'm beginning to understand how a kept man must feel."

"Why? I'll plan the wedding. Don't tell me you want to do that?"

"Not by any stretch of the imagination," he answered dryly.

She got up and went inside to grab a cordless phone, which she brought out to the porch. She sat and began to punch numbers. While she did, he reached over again to play with her hair.

She heard her mother's voice and greeted her. "Mom, I have some news," Savannah said, turning to look at him. Mike arched a brow and idly stroked her nape. His casual touches were disturbing. "I'm getting ready to enter into a new business arrangement," she said quietly, and Mike's brows arched. "I want to come tell you and Dad about it…."

She paused and then, "No, I'm still partners with Troy. This is different from my law practice. I want you and dad—and the family—to meet my new partner, actually, fiancé. Mom, I'm getting married."

Four

Sitting a few feet from her, Mike could hear voices on the other end of the line while Savannah tried to answer questions. In minutes she covered the mouthpiece of the phone. "My family wants us to come talk to them about this tonight."

"It's fine with me," Mike replied, wondering what he had gotten himself into.

An hour later, outside Stallion Pass, they drove up a long, winding drive to a sprawling two-story house nestled between large oaks with a fenced yard surrounding the house. There was a barn and several outbuildings nearby, and a corral and track visible.

Mike tried to sort out the relatives he was meeting. Everyone was talking at once and gave him strange looks. Little children were in the house, greeting him and then scattering to play in other rooms, returning to talk to a parent every few minutes. All of the adults were in the family room of her parents' house, a room with knotty pine paneling, furniture covered in floral patterns and shelves filled with books, pictures and trophies. Toys littered tables and some of the chairs.

The first chance the adults had to shoo children out of the room, Savannah's father closed the door and turned to her. "You can't marry this stranger, even if it is absolutely a business deal," Matt Clay said as if Mike wasn't sitting next to his daughter on the couch. "You don't know anything about him."

"I have a world of information on his background, and all of you know that John entrusted him with Jessie," Savannah replied.

As they talked, Mike remained silent. He could see little resemblance in Savannah's blond beauty to her father's dark-brown hair and hazel eyes.

"Savannah, you can't save the world," her father argued. "There are millions of babies who need someone. Don't do this."

"Dad, how can you of all people say that!" she snapped, and her father's face flushed.

"I want to take care of Jessie," she went on. "I want to give this little girl what you gave me." Savannah looked at her father and then turned to her mother.

"That was different, Savannah," her mother replied in a soft voice, shooting Mike worried glances.

If he'd had two heads or come from Mars, Mike didn't think they would have more objections. He studied her mother. Amy Clay had none of her daughter's beauty, either. Sandy-haired, brown-eyed and freckled, she had no distinctive features and was several inches shorter than Savannah, whose height he guessed was about five foot ten.

The storm of protests swirled around him while Savannah capably dealt with her family.

"Does this family want John's little baby to become a ward of the state?" Savannah demanded, looking at her siblings.

"He could have appointed you or one of us as her guardian, and he didn't," said Lucius, Savannah's oldest brother. "John Frates deserves what he gets here."

"Jessie doesn't," Savannah said quietly. "I know what I'm doing. Mike is giving me half the money and the house, so there will be no financial hardship."

Matt Clay looked at Mike, and Mike gazed steadily back into hazel eyes that were fiery with anger. Mike could feel the anger from all the males in the room. They didn't frighten him, and he understood their position, but he wondered why he was putting himself through something he didn't want in the first place.

"Dad," Savannah said, crossing the room to crouch in front of her father's chair. "I'm doing something I really want to do, and you're not going to talk me out of it. Now start being hospitable to Mike. He's agreeing to this so I can have what I want."

A tense silence hung over the room while Matt Clay glared at Mike. When finally he nodded, the women started talking, peppering Savannah with questions. Moments later, the women, including Savannah, left the room to look at a calendar and make plans. As soon as they were gone, Savannah's brothers exchanged looks.

"Let me show you around the place," Lucius said, standing. He was a tall, rawboned man, his skin deeply tanned by the Texas sunshine, his thick blond hair bleached almost white.

Mike followed Lucius into the backyard with its brightly lit swimming pool. Faith, the youngest sister, sat watching children splash in the pool. She merely glanced at the men and smiled.

Lucius turned to Mike. "Savannah seems to really want this sham marriage because she wants the baby, but she doesn't know much about you, does she?" he asked.

"She knows a lot more about me than I do about her," Mike answered evenly, knowing from the first few minutes that Savannah's brothers were ready to protect their sister's interests.

"Yeah, maybe," Lucius said, "but basically, you're two strangers. I want you to know—and I'm speaking for Andy and Jacob, too—we don't want to see her hurt. You understand?"

"Absolutely," Mike said, holding his temper, because he knew that her family had good reason to be suspicious of a stranger marrying their sister in a name-only union. "I think Savannah is capable of taking care of herself, too."

He gazed into cold, green eyes and could feel the tension tighten between them.

"Maybe she can, but I want you to be careful."

"Don't worry about your sister. I have no intention of hurting her, and she's getting what she wants."

"She deserves better than this," Lucius said, frowning.

"I agree with you, but this is what she wants to do."

"Why the hell are *you* doing this? You're giving her half the money and the house. Everybody wants something. What do you want out of this?"

Mike took a deep breath, still hanging on tenuously to his temper. "Not a damn thing, other than peace of mind. She wants that little baby desperately. It won't hurt me to give Savannah time and my name until she can legally adopt Jessie." He paused. "Look, Lucius, I don't want to do this. I have my life and I like my independence. This paper marriage is putting a crimp in my plans. I'm just trying to do a good deed here, so don't push too hard."

Lucius Clay's chest expanded as he inhaled and clenched his fists. Mike clenched his, wondering if the guy, who was a good three inches taller than he was, planned to take a swing at him.

"Lucius!" Savannah came striding out of the house and hurried over to them. She linked her arm through Mike's, and he forgot about Lucius, inhaling her perfume and intensely aware of her pressed against his side. He knew she was doing it in an effort to calm Lucius, and for the benefit of her family, but Mike liked having her close.

"You leave my fiancé alone," she said to her brother. "I can imagine this conversation. C'mon, Mike. Mom is serving peach cobbler now and we've got a wedding date set." As Savannah talked, she tugged on his arm and he turned to walk with her back to the house.

"Maybe you saved me from getting pounded," he said, placing his arm across her shoulders, knowing she would not push him away.

She smiled at him. "With your background, you could pulverize Lucius. He's a cowboy, not a trained fighter."

"I'd never underestimate a cowboy. I think your dad and your brothers are ready to hang me from the nearest tree. Your family is giving me looks I would have expected if I had dropped here from Mars."

She smiled. "They'll accept you. They just need time. And needless to say, the women like you—but you know that."

"Not your mom. I saw the looks she gave me, too. She doesn't want you to do this, either, does she."

"No, she doesn't, but she knows I'm capable of making my own decisions, so she'll support me in what I want to do."

"Yeah, well, your menfolk have mayhem on their minds."

She smiled up at him. "I'm not worried. You're not scared of them, and I know you can take care of yourself."

"I hope it doesn't come to that."

"It won't. They'll do what I want. And our arrangement will stay within our families. As far as friends are concerned, it will be better if everyone thinks I've fallen in love."

"Okay," he said, "but in addition to family, I want to level with the two other guys you had in your office—Jonah and Boone. They're almost as close as my brothers, and they'll be around some because of John's will—at least until they dispose of their inheritances. I want them to know the truth. I want Colin Garrick's family to know, too. I'm close with them.''

''That's fine. I heard about Colin from John. He changed the will when Colin was killed.''

He looked down at her and wondered if they could convince anyone they were in love.

They entered a kitchen filled with dripping children and Savannah's parents and brothers. He was served a generous helping of warm cobbler and ice cream, and they sat around a long table, conversation flowing around him with lots of laughter, yet he frequently caught Lucius or one of her other brothers giving him a cold, hard look.

While they ate he had time to sort out parents and children. Lucius had two towheaded boys. Savannah's oldest sister, Helen, was a curly-haired, brown-eyed blonde with three boys. Andy, black hair in a buzz cut, had two boys and a girl. The next sister in age was auburn-haired Jovita, who had a boy and a girl. Jacob had a baby boy. The youngest sibling, Faith, looked like Amy Clay and had a toddler. Mike knew it would take another visit to get the kids' names straight.

Later, when Mike and Savannah walked to her car to go home, he held out his hand. ''Give me the keys. I'll drive back.''

To his surprise she handed him the keys without a protest. He held the door for her and then went around to slide behind the wheel. As they drove away, she waved to her family, who stood outside and waved in return.

''They see you like a lamb going to the slaughter,'' Mike said.

''They'll get used to this.''

''Will you and I?'' he asked, filled with strong doubts, in spite of his reassurances to her family.

"Of course," Savannah replied firmly. She placed her hand on his knee. "You were great. Thanks."

Mike inhaled sharply. He had been out of the country and obviously too long without a woman, because every smile from Savannah, every touch, had too big an effect on him. He covered her hand with his, glancing at her, and she smiled.

"We're doing all right," she said, pulling her hand away, but he caught it and placed it back on his knee.

"I like your hand on me," he said.

"You surprise me."

"It's marriage that worries me. We're getting married three weeks from Saturday," he said, feeling butterflies in his stomach at the thought.

"You said that would fit your schedule," she reminded him.

"It will. I'll go back to D.C. tomorrow and leave the planning to you."

"This will be a whirlwind. I wish for Jessie's sake it could be sooner, but three weeks is record-setting for a big wedding like we'll have."

At her condo, she switched on lights and turned to him. "Want to have a cold drink and talk about the prenup agreement now?"

"Relax," Mike said, amused by her charging full throttle into this marriage. "You can work on the prenup tomorrow or the next day," he said. "Let's have a cold drink and talk. We're going to share a house, share our lives, share a baby. We ought to know a little more about each other."

"I'd think after the last few hours with my family, you'd have had all of me you could stand. Besides, that's procrastination. We have to get a prenup agreement."

"I still can't believe you're doing this."

"I know when you made the suggestion, you didn't think I would," she said, her eyes twinkling with mischief. "You aren't backing out, are you?"

He took a deep breath. "I want to back out, but if I did, I might have trouble living with that decision. Not to mention your family would skin me alive. So I'll go through with it for one year."

"It's not going to take a year of your life," she answered, and the sparkle in her eyes changed to fire. "I'll start adoption proceedings immediately. Of course, the adoption will go smoother if you and I both do it, since we'll be legally wed."

"I understand that. Then I'm out of here and I'll get my life back on track."

"I hope the three of you are happy."

"Three of us?"

"Sure—me, myself and I. That's all that concerns you," she said, looking up at him.

"Dammit, I'm giving you what you want and tearing up my life to do it!"

She turned away swiftly. "Thank you for doing that much," she said.

Annoyed, he caught her arm and pulled her around to face him. "Stop pushing or I'll go, and to hell with any wedding plans."

As she gazed up at him, her face flushed. Both of them were breathing hard, and his anger boiled beneath the surface. Yet even with anger stirring both of them, when he touched her and stood close, looking into her blue eyes, he knew his racing pulse wasn't all due to anger. He couldn't resist looking at her full lips, remembering the kiss that had tied him in knots and made him want more. In spite of his anger, he wanted to kiss her now.

With a twist she yanked her arm away. "Let's get our drinks and then start the prenuptial agreement," she said, turning to get glasses and fill them with ice.

For the next few hours, they talked and Savannah made notes, determined to get the prenuptial agreement sketched out while he was with her so they would have it done. It was four in the morning when Mike said he was turning in. Savannah walked down the hall with him. At his door he turned to face her.

"Well, you're getting your way," he said. "Congratulations."

"Thanks for going along with it. It was your idea, after all."

"Right," he said. She turned and headed to her room, glancing back over her shoulder at him before she disappeared.

Three weeks later on Saturday morning, Mike was more dazed than ever. In the living room of Savannah's parents' home, he stood with his brother Jake beside him as best man. His youngest brother, Sam, was a groomsman along with Mike's military buddies, Boone and Jonah, and Colin Garrick's younger brother, Kevin. At least they all knew the real reason he was tying the knot.

Mike stood waiting, his palms sweaty. He couldn't believe they were actually going through with this wedding, yet here they were, joined by a houseful of guests, surrounded with candles and flowers and music he barely heard.

For the past three weeks he had made constant trips back and forth between D.C. and Texas, getting ready for his new life. Since he'd had to postpone joining the CIA, he'd decided to open his own security business in Texas. Just two days earlier he and Savannah had gone to get little Jessie, signing papers and going through formalities. For a few brief moments, the baby was placed in his arms, and he gazed down at the sleeping child. Mike had been awed by her, still amazed that she was his charge, although Savannah would step in and relieve him of that soon. He looked at the curly strands of wispy brown hair, smooth, pink skin. Her tiny hands were folded over her tummy. And for the first time, he felt good about the marriage. He couldn't take the tyke as his forever, but to give her this opportunity in life, he could take a year and change his plans a bit.

He had glanced up to find Savannah watching him. She crossed the room to take Jessie from his arms and place her in the baby carrier.

Mike had picked up the carrier and secured it in his new four-door sedan, and then they drove to Savannah's parents' home, where her mother would keep Jessie until after the wedding.

At the church now, the baby was in a carrier on a pew beside Savannah's mother, who seemed as taken with the baby as Savannah. The family had hovered over the little girl, and if there was ever a group of people who loved babies and children, Savannah's family was it, Mike realized.

He didn't know a thing about caring for a baby, but it wouldn't matter. Savannah would make up for his lack.

The organ and violins signaled the entrance of the bride, bringing his thoughts back to the moment. Mike gazed across the church.

As Savannah walked toward him, he forgot everything else. His breath caught in his throat and he couldn't stop staring at her.

Savannah was a beautiful woman, but today, she was stunning. She positively glowed, the white dress emphasizing her tiny waist and full breasts. The sleeves barely covered her shoulders and her skin was flawless. Her golden hair was looped and pinned high beneath a thin veil that fell over the back of her head. Whatever his future held, Mike knew that for the rest of his life, he would remember the way Savannah looked at this moment. No woman could possibly be more beautiful. If he ever had a real wedding, a real love, his bride couldn't be more gorgeous and alluring than Savannah was right now.

His heart thudded as he looked into blue eyes that sparkled with happiness. Not a touch of uncertainty showed in her features. A slight smile curved her full red lips. Her chin was tilted up, and once again he thought what foolishness she was committing. She should have waited for real love. She should be doing this with a man who adored her.

In addition to her bouquet of white orchids, white roses, baby's breath and stephanotis, Savannah carried two long-stemmed red roses, one of which she gave to each mother, giving her own mother a brief kiss on the cheek along with the rose. He knew his family had mixed feelings about the union. His parents were still happy and hoped he would stay married while his brothers thought he was giving up his freedom. Then her gaze went to Mike as she approached him.

The minute Mike looked into Savannah's eyes, he wanted her with an intensity that shook him.

When her father placed her hand in Mike's, his fingers closed around her warm hand, and she gazed up at him with shining eyes.

As he repeated his vows, Mike again wondered what he had gotten himself into. Still, this union was only temporary, he reminded himself. He wondered what ran through Savannah's mind. From the happiness radiating from her expression, she couldn't be entertaining the doubts he was.

Savannah repeated her vows, knowing they weren't true, but keeping in mind little Jessie and all the child would get from this union. Gazing up at Mike, Savannah thought he looked pale, in spite of his tan. Worry clouded his brown eyes, and she knew he was wishing he were a million miles away from this marriage ceremony, which was real even if their marriage was not; yet at the same time how handsome he looked! Excitement bubbled in her and she knew that he, along with Jessie, was the cause.

"You may kiss the bride," the minister said.

Mike slipped his arm around her waist and leaned forward, his lips brushing hers so casually, yet the effect was far from light. The moment his mouth touched hers, she tingled from head to toe. She looked up into dark eyes that held no clues to what he was feeling, but a muscle flexed in his jaw, and she suspected he was unhappy.

She brushed aside concerns because she was married now and Jessie was theirs—hers, really.

Savannah wanted wedding pictures to save for Jessie later. When Mike got the divorce and went out of their lives, he was still going to be Jessie's legal father, so Savannah wanted pictures to show her child. *Her child.* The words were magic, and she knew that every moment of this sham marriage would be worth it. She was grateful to Mike for the upheaval he'd been willing to undergo in his life. And she would try to avoid thinking about any *what if*s or *if only*s.

As they posed for the photographer with the wedding party, Savannah linked her arm with Mike's. When he arched his brows, she smiled up at him.

Finally they were in the limo headed to the Stallion Pass Country Club for the reception which included a larger number of guests. Mike twisted in the seat to look at her. "Well, you did it. We're legally husband and wife now."

She reached over to take his hand and squeeze it, and his fingers closed around hers instantly. "Thank you. You've made so many changes, Mike. Thank you for all of them."

He shrugged one shoulder as he gazed back at her. "It wasn't that big of a sacrifice. Put off the CIA for a while. Who knows, maybe I'll like the security business. Now, a small town—Stallion Pass—that's going to take more of an adjustment. At least my new business is in San Antonio. I doubt if Stallion Pass has much crime."

She laughed, feeling giddy and excited because of the handsome man sitting nearby, his dark tux complementing his deep tan.

"Why the roses for our mothers today?" he asked. "This wedding is just for convenience."

"To me, our marriage is important. I get Jessie and you enabled that, so I'm grateful to you, and your family is part of you. Besides, I told your mother that she should consider Jessie her granddaughter, and since she never had a daughter or a granddaughter, she seems excited. My mother already knows this is a special occasion."

"Dammit, Savannah, you shouldn't have settled for such a half-baked deal." He frowned at her. "You should have waited and gotten the whole thing with a guy you love, a guy who adores you. You could have had your own babies."

She shook her head. "I'm happy. I have what I want."

"I hope it doesn't jump up and bite you. Little Jessie may not turn out like you think she will."

"You're not putting a damper on this wonderful day!" she said, extracting her hand from his.

He looked exasperated before he turned to stare out the window, and she felt shut out of his life and wondered if he was still angry over the whole plan.

Then they pulled up in front of the club and exited the limo. Mike took her hand and they swept into the entryway with its gleaming hardwood floor and enormous crystal chandelier.

In the large ballroom, a string quartet was already playing. "I'm surprised your father gave us such an extravagant wedding," Mike said. "He would cheerfully wring my neck if it wouldn't make you unhappy." He looked at the lavish buffet, which surrounded an ice-castle sculpture. One end of the room was filled with round tables covered with white linen tablecloths centered with vases of pink roses. Near one wall two rectangular tables held a six-tier white bride's cake and a three-tier chocolate groom's cake. Waiters moved around the room serving champagne, while punch was served at one of the tables.

"My father loves me—that's why the big wedding. His feelings for you don't weigh in the decisions about our wedding,'' she said, and then smiled as friends came to greet her.

In minutes Mike was as busy as Savannah, talking with his friends and other wedding guests. He shook hands with many of Savannah's friends and her family's friends. A vaguely familiar-looking man stepped up to shake his hand—Troy Slocum, Savannah's partner. Mike was surprised at the chill in the man's eyes.

"Congratulations," Troy said. His voice lacked sincerity. "You came to town and swept Savannah off her feet. I hope you both are happy," he added stiffly.

"Thanks, Mr. Slocum," Mike answered, feeling the animosity emanating from the man.

"It's Troy. You and I will see a lot of each other, I'm sure. Congratulations again. You have a wonderful woman for your wife."

"Thanks," Mike answered. As another person stepped up to congratulate him, Troy moved away.

The reception was a blur of new names and faces that Mike knew he wouldn't remember, but there were exceptions, particularly when Savannah motioned to him to join her as she stood talking to two couples.

"Mike, I want you to meet my friends, Grace and Wyatt Sawyer," Savannah said, and Mike shook hands with an attractive red-haired woman and a tall black-haired man. Savannah turned to the couple on her left. "And this is Laurie and Josh Kellogg."

Mike received warm smiles and greetings from a striking couple.

"Josh and Wyatt are ranchers, and we've all known each other forever," Savannah said.

"Congratulations," Wyatt told him. "Savannah's special, but I don't have to tell you that. And watch out for her practical jokes. I probably don't have to warn you about those, though."

Unable to imagine Savannah letting go enough to play a practical joke, Mike arched his eyebrows as she shrugged.

"Jessie is an adorable little girl," Grace said.

"But then, Grace thinks all children are adorable," Wyatt added, and they all laughed.

"I think that description fits my new wife, too," Mike said.

"Well, it fits mine," Josh declared, smiling at Laurie.

"Do you have pictures?" Savannah asked, and in a few seconds, Mike was passed pictures of Wyatt's two—Megan and a new baby, Ryan. Then he looked at pictures of the Kelloggs' little girl, Sophie.

"We'll all get together sometime and let these little kids play," Grace said as Wyatt put the pictures back into his billfold.

When a band replaced the string quartet and began to play, Mike turned to Savannah. "I think that's our cue," he said, taking her hand. "If y'all will excuse us," he said to the Kelloggs and the Sawyers before he led Savannah to the dance floor.

Taking her into his arms to dance, he looked down at her. She had fastened up the long train of her dress and removed her veil. "I haven't told you yet—you look gorgeous, Savannah."

Her heart lurched and she drew a quick breath, smiling up at him and telling herself he was just being polite. "Thank you. And you look quite handsome."

"Thanks. So we're going to try to get along in this new arrangement we have?"

"I don't see why not."

"I'm still amazed you took me up on the idea. I think you cheated yourself," he said quietly, his gaze going over her features as they danced. She was aware of being in his arms, of the scent of his aftershave, of his dark gaze on her.

"I'm supremely happy," she said, smiling up at him. "Every one of my friends thinks we're wildly in love."

Mike watched her while they danced. "There are moments when there are sparks between us. I guess it shows."

"There are sparks, all right, like little explosions of dynamite."

"You know what I'm talking about," he said in a softer voice, tightening his arm around her waist and pulling her closer. "Your pulse is racing right now."

She slanted him a saucy look. "Maybe it's due to wedding excitement and champagne."

Mike tightened his arm again and brought her other hand against his chest, holding her close while they danced. "You like playing with fire," he whispered in her ear. "I'm burning up, and it isn't from the wedding or the champagne. And I don't think those are causing your pulse to race, either. When we're alone, I'll show you," he promised.

His breath in her ear tickled. Savannah knew she was flirting with him, and it was as dangerous as taunting a tiger, yet impossible to resist.

"Don't hold me quite so close," she whispered. "Right now we ought to do what's proper."

"This *is* proper for newlyweds. Matter of fact, it may take that murderous gleam out of your brothers' and father's eyes when they look at me. If they think there's a chance we'll fall in love, they might stop harboring thoughts of doing me in."

"So that's why you're dancing close," she said, suddenly annoyed with him.

He looked down at her, a faint smile on his face. "No, it's not why I'm holding you close. I'm tempted to kiss you and see what that does to your pulse, but I'd rather save the kiss for when there's only the two of us."

Savannah's pulse was racing. She wished it wasn't and she wished he didn't know that she reacted to him so strongly.

"Remember, this is a paper wedding of two people who barely know each other," she said.

"I intend to get to know the long-legged, beautiful blonde who is now my wife much better."

"I didn't know you noticed."

"Like hell you didn't," he said, smiling. "You know the effect you have on me."

She smiled in return. "At least we have a truce," she replied, but anger and snap faded and her voice was breathless.

"Definitely! Today—and tonight—we'll learn all about each other. Your folks have Jessie while we fly out of here later and spend tonight in New Orleans. It'll be a real date."

"I didn't know you were interested," she said, tilting her head to study him.

"I'm interested, Savannah. I tried to get you out on a date that second day, remember? You wouldn't go."

"It's different now. Only, don't be too charming, Mike," she said solemnly, meaning it.

"Why not?"

"I'd hate to fall in love with you, because I know you'll be out of my life as soon as we get things worked out."

"Come on, Savannah. You've had relationships before and survived them, and so have I. Let's enjoy each other's company."

"I'm all for that," she said, realizing the words she had said to him were too true. She didn't want to fall in love with her handsome new husband, because he would not love her in return.

As he spun her around, she said, "I'll bet your past is strewn with broken hearts."

He shrugged one broad shoulder. "I'll bet there are some in *your* past, too. Let's forget days gone by. I want to know what makes you feel good and what you're like when you lose control. I want more kisses from you. I haven't forgotten the kisses we've shared. Have you forgotten, Savannah?" he asked softly. As his brown gaze bore into her, she felt her cheeks flush and knew he had his answer without her saying a word.

The music ended and he held both of her hands, still watching her.

"I dance with my father next and you with your mother," Savannah said, but her mind was still on all Mike had told her.

"Tonight will be special," he said softly, leaning down to brush a kiss across her cheek. Guests applauded, and Mike smiled at her. "My brothers can't wait to claim a dance. They know our arrangement, but I've warned them, they better not hit on you."

She laughed. "Go find your mother. Your brothers have been charming."

Savannah's father crossed the room to her, and Mike left to find his mother and lead her onto the dance floor.

"You looked happy out here just now with Mike," her father said to Savannah as they danced. There was curiosity in his expression.

"I am happy. Mike is nice, Dad. And I'm definitely getting what I want."

"He better not hurt you, Savannah. I think you deserve a lot more than a loveless marriage." He tilted his head to look at her. "Maybe you two will fall in love. Make it a marriage for real."

"Maybe we will," she said, smiling at her father, knowing that no such thing would happen but wanting her family to accept Mike and her brothers to stop threatening him.

"If he ever causes you trouble, I want you to promise that you'll let us know."

She laughed. "Dad, you'd think I was marrying a monster!"

"He's a tough man, Savannah. It shows."

"Stop worrying. I'm supremely happy," she said, a fluttery feeling in the pit of her stomach. Things weren't the best ever, but still they were what she wanted.

"Be careful," Matt Clay warned.

"I will," she promised, but she didn't know how to stop her heart from responding to Mike.

It was midafternoon before they could get away, making a dash to the waiting limousine and being driven to her sister Helen's empty house, where Savannah rushed inside and changed from her wedding dress to a simple blue sheath that ended just above her knees. In minutes she was back in the limo with Mike, and soon they were onboard a flight to New Orleans.

Five

On the top floor of an elegant hotel along the Riverwalk, Mike had reserved a suite for Savannah and a room next to the suite for him. When they followed a bellman into the suite, Mike tipped him while Savannah crossed to the windows to look out at the Mississippi, where the sunset sent streamers of fire across the wide ribbon of water.

As soon as the door closed, Mike said, "I want to change out of this tux." His words were calm, but emotions churned in him and doubts plagued him. Yet at the same time, each day he was with Savannah, he wanted her more, and tonight they would have a real date. "Give me ten minutes," he said. "I have dinner reservations for us."

She nodded, and he picked up his suitcase and left. While he was gone, she changed into a black, silk sleeveless dress with a straight, knee-length skirt.

She opened the door minutes later to find Mike standing there in a navy suit and tie. His gaze went over her appreciatively.

"You look as beautiful as ever, and I'm glad you left your hair down."

Pleased, she smiled at him as she closed the door behind her. He took her arm and they left for dinner at a restaurant in the French Quarter. The cool night air was invigorating. The sound of a trumpet carried along the street and the man beside her added to Savannah's exuberance.

When they were seated at a table covered with a white linen cloth, the waiter took their drink order and left.

"I still can't believe this is happening," Savannah said, thinking Mike looked just as handsome in his suit as he had in his tux.

"It's official, Savannah," he said.

"But not permanent."

"You got what you wanted, and actually, I like that I can take you out on a date now."

"You're so sure…" she began, pausing when their waiter returned with two glasses of white wine.

"Sure of what?" Mike prompted when they were alone again.

"That you won't fall in love," she finished.

"Who knows where this marriage will lead us?" he said lightly, but she knew what his true answer was. He raised his glass of wine.

"Here's to our partnership. May it not be lions and tigers all the time."

Smiling at him, she touched his glass with hers before she sipped, watching him over the rim. When she set her glass down, she wiggled her fingers. "The ring is beautiful," she said, looking at the diamond he'd given her on his last return from Washington, D.C. It sparkled in the soft light.

Mike's tanned fingers closed around her hand. "The hand that's wearing it is what's pretty." He turned her hand in his, lightly rubbing his thumb back and forth along her wrist, a casual touch but electrifying.

Feeling closer to him than anytime before, she touched a pale scar that sliced across the back of his hand. "What happened here?"

"That one I got when a man came at me with a knife," he answered nonchalantly.

Unable to imagine the life he had led, she shivered. "It's a good thing you're out of the military. Do you think you'll miss it?"

His eyes clouded over, and she knew she had entered a sensitive area even though he replied, "No, I'm thankful to be out. Civilian life looks good. And now I have a new wife and a new business."

"Not a real wife," she said softly.

"A very real woman and one I want to get to know. I want to know what's beneath that cool control you always show."

She smiled. "I'm happy to hear that you think I've been practicing control. The trouble is, you're too accustomed to getting your way," she said.

"I won't get my way tonight," he said quietly.

"Now what do you want—seduction?"

He leaned closer to her over the table. "I'll show you at the hotel."

"You're a dangerous man, Mike. I'll have to guard my heart. I'm grateful to you for what you're doing, but I'm not giving you my body or my soul out of gratitude."

He cocked one dark eyebrow. "Always a challenge from you, Savannah." He raised her hand and kissed her palm, slowly, lingering, his tongue touching it while he watched her.

She was drowning in the dark pools of his eyes, and she knew he was aware of her racing pulse. "You know how I react to you. There's no hiding that or changing it."

"And that makes you irresistible," he said softly.

When the waiter appeared with their dinners, Mike leaned back and released her hand. Plates of roasted pepper-crusted salmon and braised spinach were set before them, but Savannah found her appetite had fled.

It was early when they returned to the hotel.

"I ordered champagne to be sent up. Want to have some now and celebrate a little longer?" Mike asked.

"Against my good judgment…come in, Mike."

"Good judgment? I can't be a threat now."

She gave him a look over her shoulder as he followed her into the suite and closed the door behind him.

Savannah watched him as he stepped into the suite, and she could well imagine him doing the tough job he'd had to do in Special Forces. He moved with a lithe ease, a contained power. He was aware of everything around him. She had been with him enough now to know that. In the French Quarter, while he was charming and attentive to her, she knew he was completely aware of his surroundings.

Turning on a light in the small adjoining kitchen, he switched on music and opened the draperies, pulling a pair of padded chairs close to the windows so they could enjoy the lights of the city reflected in the dark waters of the river. Still standing, Savannah took in the view for a moment, then turned to look at Mike. She found him more fascinating.

He opened the champagne and poured two glasses of the pale, bubbly liquid, then handed one to her. "Happy future to my bride."

"Thanks, Mike. Happy future to you, too."

"I hope it works out for you and Jessie."

"I expect it to. As soon as we get home, I want to start the adoption proceedings, because sometimes they take a lot of time."

"It's fine with me. That's what we planned to do. Let's sit," he said, gesturing at the chairs. He placed his champagne flute on the table and took off his tie, draping it over the back of a chair. He shed his coat and folded it over the same chair. Watching him, Savannah's breath altered. Was she going to be able to keep her guard up around this sexy man?

Turning, he saw her watching him, and her face flushed. She sat, crossing her legs and looking at the view, yet totally conscious of him as he sat, too. The deep maroon chairs swiveled, and Mike turned his, almost knocking knees with her.

"Thank heavens we've hired a nanny," she said, thinking of Constance McGrath, the young woman Savannah had hired last week. "This isn't a good time for me to miss work."

"Do you have a big case coming up?"

"Yes. It's a civil case involving a drilling company and an oil company, and each one thinks the other cheated them. We represent the oil company, who is the defendant." She was acutely conscious of Mike sitting so close to her, his gaze lingering on her mouth. Mike reached over to tangle his fingers in her hair, letting locks of it slide through his fingers, his hand lightly caressing her nape. Then he took her drink and set it on the table beside them.

Savannah could barely think about the office, because Mike sat so close. His fingers brushed her nape, playing in her hair. Through the wedding and the reception and throughout the evening, they had touched, danced together, flirted, every contact fanning the attraction that smoldered between them.

"Remember I told you that we make each other's pulses race?" His hand slipped around to touch her throat lightly. "I can feel your pulse, and it's speeding now."

"Is yours?" she asked, touching his throat.

"Mine has been breaking records since the moment you walked down the aisle. No woman ever looked as beautiful as you did, Savannah," he said in a husky voice, leaning forward to brush light kisses over her ear and her throat.

His seductive words added to the spell he was weaving. She was ensnared, caught in a current she couldn't resist.

He took her hand and stood. "Come here, Savannah."

Looking into his eyes, she knew his intent, and her heartbeat accelerated another notch. As she stood, he slipped his arm around her waist. "I've been wanting to do this all day," he said.

He leaned down, and his mouth covered hers. The first touch was electrifying.

His arm tightened around her, pulling her against his hard length as he leaned over her and kissed her deeply. Wanting him, she wound her arms around his neck, her fingers tangling in his hair while she returned his plundering kisses, heightening the fire that already consumed her.

Savannah clung to him, kissing him hungrily, knowing no man had ever made her tremble with such need. No man's kisses had ever set her so aflame. Perspiration beaded her brow, and she could barely get her breath and soon kisses weren't enough. Every stroke of his tongue built a need that was already raging.

When his hand slipped down her back and over her bottom, desire shook her profoundly. She wanted this tough warrior who kept his heart locked away. She brought her hands to his broad chest, leaning away to unbutton his shirt. And then she touched his warm, rock-hard chest, trailing her fingers over sculpted muscles, feeling small ridges of scar tissue, tiny reminders of the kind of man he was.

Mike caressed her nape, stroking her and easing down the zipper of her dress. When he pushed the silky material away, cool air spilled over her bare shoulders.

Mike leaned away to look at her, and she trembled beneath his gaze, the desire in his dark eyes one more fiery touch that heightened her need. His hands cupped her breasts, his thumbs drawing lazy circles over her nipples, driving her wild.

As he unfastened the clasp of her bra and pushed away the lace to cup her breasts again, she moaned softly. "You're beautiful," he whispered before he leaned down to take her nipple into his mouth, to gently tease and torment.

"Mike," she gasped, holding his shoulders. She ran her fingers through his hair.

He groaned, hauling her into his embrace, his arms closing tightly around her as he kissed her again, a demanding kiss that possessed and made her feel he wanted to devour her. She was crushed against him, and she felt his thick shaft and knew he wanted her.

Also, she knew she had to stop him now or there would be no stopping, and Mike was going too far, too fast. Torn with conflicting emotions, she didn't want to stop, either. She wanted him with an urgency that surprised her. It was difficult to think, to do anything except cling to him and kiss him in return. He tugged his shirt away, tossing it aside, and then she was pressed against his bare chest.

Clinging to him, she moved her hips against him, kissing him passionately while her blood thundered in her ears. For a few more moments she ignored the emotional battle raging within her.

"Mike," she whispered finally, pushing against his shoulder and then wriggling away slightly. "Mike, you're going too fast." She pushed against his chest.

He raised his head to look at her, a look that scalded and took her breath away. He made no effort to hide his blatant desire. He trailed his fingertips across her bare breasts. She gasped, trembling while tingles shot through her, then settled low in her belly, pooling into hot desire. Gasping for breath, she yanked up her dress to cover herself.

"We can't go this fast."

"Why not?" he asked, his voice husky. "We're husband and wife, after all."

"Not really, and you know it!" she snapped, on edge because she had lost control, and he had stirred her more than she had dreamed possible. And he stood only inches away, bare-chested, broad-shouldered, his stomach a washboard of muscles. She had to fight to keep from staring at his body. "I'm not ready for this. We have a business arrangement, that's all."

"That isn't all," he answered quietly, resting his hand on her shoulder and toying with her hair. "You kissed me back. You want what I want. You respond to me, Savannah."

"All right, I'll admit that I do, but logic says slow down. I'm not hopping into your bed tonight when this has been the first real date we've had."

"All right, Savannah," he said quietly, stepping close and tucking her hair behind her ears. He reached behind her to tug her zipper up, pulling it slowly, all the time gazing into her eyes with that hungry look that made her feel totally desirable, totally beautiful.

"We can sit and talk and get to know each other tonight if that's what you want," he said. "We can take more time, but ultimately I want you in my bed."

She placed her fingers on his lips. "Stop it!" she said fiercely. "You're trying to seduce me right now with your talk of wanting me."

"Not so. I'm telling you my intentions and desires, desires that aren't one way. You're trying to hold on to that ever-present logic of yours, pulling it around you like a cloak, but you want to make love, too. For a few minutes there, you let go. Deny that one, Savannah."

"We have a *business* arrangement. I don't want to be a toy for your amusement for the next twelve months, and then you pack up and leave."

"I was thinking of something that was mutually satisfying, not just *my* entertainment," he said.

"You're thinking of something purely physical, and that's not what I want. If there is a physical relationship, then there has to be emotional involvement if you expect to include me."

"What you say and what you do are two different things," he chided, running his fingers lightly along her cheek. "You like to kiss, and I'm going to get you to let go completely. You already half want to."

"Watch out or you'll get yourself into something permanent," she threatened.

Aware of her challenge and another clash of wills, he shook his head. "When the year is up, I will walk, no matter what happens in between."

She smiled at him, looking into his eyes and feeling sparks fly. He slipped his hand behind her head. "I mean it," he said. "I'm leaving when a year has passed."

"I didn't argue with you."

"The look you gave me was argument enough."

"We should say good night and call it an evening," she said, stepping away from him.

"Nonsense. It's our wedding night. We can at least talk and sip the champagne. Sit down and tell me about your life."

She stood staring at him, once again torn between wanting to sit and talk and knowing she should get him out of her room now. He tugged lightly on her hand.

"Sit down. I won't bite."

"I'm not afraid of a bite," she said, sitting and crossing her legs.

"Don't tell me you're afraid of my kisses. I didn't think there was an ounce of fear in you a few minutes ago. Or are you afraid of seduction?" he asked softly. "Or are you afraid of yourself?"

"I knew we should call it a night," she said, starting to get up, but he caught her arm.

"Sit down. I promise we'll just talk." He picked up the champagne flutes, handing one to her.

Exasperated with him, and herself, she stared at him a moment, then asked him about his brothers and their careers. As he talked, she watched Mike stretch out his long legs and cross them at the ankles. He looked relaxed, as if the kisses had never happened, while she was tied in knots, tingling and aching enough that she had to fight the temptation to reach for him. How was she going to survive this bargain marriage without succumbing to his charm?

Once, after they had lapsed into a brief silence, Mike asked, "Remember that first night we went to your family's house? When your dad told you that you couldn't save the world, you came back with something to the effect of 'How can you, of all people, say that?'" Mike rested his elbows on his knees and his index finger traced circles on her knee while he talked. "Why him 'of all people'?"

"You're very observant, Mike," she said, too aware of his finger drawing circles on her knee.

"You said you wanted to give Jessie what they gave you. You wanted this baby desperately and you told me that you didn't know me well enough to tell me, but we know each other better now."

Savannah looked away. "It's no big secret. The four oldest of us are adopted. My parents have been wonderful, and I feel very fortunate. I just want Jessie to have that kind of life, too," she said quietly, still feeling old hurts. "When I was four years old, my father walked out on my mother and me. A little later, my mother abandoned me, too. I became a ward of the state and was shuffled from family to family."

"Damn, I'm sorry," he said. "I pried into something I shouldn't have."

She turned to look at him and shook her head. "That's all right. It's really no secret, particularly around Stallion Pass. Matt and Amy adopted me. That was the most wonderful thing that could have happened to me."

"So, some of your brothers and sisters are also adopted and some aren't. I knew you didn't look much like your mother or father."

"Mike, being abandoned by my biological parents was devastating. And then I was just shuffled from one home to another. Too many nights for a long time, I cried myself to sleep. So yes, you're right. I had a deeper reason to fight for Jessie," she said stiffly.

"Savannah," he said quietly. "I'm sorry I brought the matter up. Jessie's yours now and with your family to help, she'll have great care and plenty of love."

They talked a while longer, and then Mike stood. "Come tell me good night. I'll turn in now." He caught her hand and pulled her to her feet. "Mrs. Michael Remington. It amazes me. You got what you wanted, Savannah. That part doesn't surprise me at all."

"It does me. I'm still stunned that you agreed to marry, but I'm glad you did."

He held her hand and they strolled to the door of the suite, where he turned to her. "One good-night kiss," he said.

She gazed up at him and shook her head. "You're incorrigible, and seductive and charming, but I'm going to resist you."

"Ah, Savannah. Temptation is the spice of life."

"It's no such thing—"

He leaned down and kissed her, catching her with her lips parted.

She was rocked by another dazzling kiss, her temperature soaring instantly and all thoughts of what she should do vanishing completely.

And then he released her. She opened her eyes to find him watching her. "Someday, I'm going to make love to you for hours on end."

"That isn't any part of the deal," she said, still trying to catch her breath and gather her wits.

"That doesn't mean it isn't going to happen. You like to kiss me."

"A few kisses do not a seduction make," she replied softly. "You're a hardhearted man, and I'm not going to forget that."

"We'll see," he said, smiling at her and touching her

cheek with his finger. "Let's have breakfast together in the morning."

Without waiting for her answer, he turned and was gone, closing the door quietly behind him, leaving her dazed, hot, bothered and trembling, wanting him yet at the same time thankful he had gone to his room.

She moved away from the door, thinking about him in bed only yards away. He would have stayed all night if she had agreed. They could live as husband and wife if she would agree.

And that was exactly what Savannah wanted to guard her heart against. Even if she lived with Mike for a year, she had no illusions about his falling in love with her and staying forever. The man was tough, hard, experienced and totally wrapped up in himself and his plans for his future.

She moved around the suite, unzipping her dress, changing to her blue silk pajamas she had worn for years, knowing when she had packed that she would be sleeping alone tonight.

Tomorrow she and Mike would have breakfast together and then fly home, and she suspected that they would go their separate ways.

Finally Savannah stretched out in bed, but sleep wouldn't come. She was still wound up from the wedding, tingly from his lovemaking, unable to get him out of her thoughts and unable to go to sleep. That night as she lay in bed, moments of the wedding and the reception spun in her mind. She thought about the Garricks' arrival last night when they were all gathered at the church for the rehearsal. An older couple had entered the church with a young man. Mike had spotted them and hurried over to greet them. Savannah had stood nearby, and she'd heard the break in Mike's voice and then to her shock, when he hugged each of the Garricks, she'd seen tears in his eyes.

He hadn't gotten teary-eyed when he'd greeted his brothers or parents, a family that was strikingly handsome.

Mike's mother, Margo, was a beautiful, black-haired woman with large, luminous brown eyes, full red lips and a full figure. His father, Dan, was tall, deeply tanned and handsome enough to be in movies, and Savannah could see where all three sons got their rugged good looks.

When Savannah had asked Mike later about the Garricks, Mike had gotten a shuttered look, gazing through her as if looking into the past. He had told her that he had felt as close to Colin Garrick as he did to his brothers, and he hated the loss. When she asked how Colin died, Mike had simply said, "In the line of duty," and changed the subject, and she knew he didn't want to talk about it, so she dropped it.

She lay in bed puzzled about Mike, who kept so much of himself shut away.

After an hour of tossing and turning, she threw back the sheet and got up to sit by the window and look out at the dark Mississippi and recall another clear memory from this week—the day before yesterday when she'd picked up Jessie.

Excitement had boiled in Savannah that night. She had been up before dawn, carefully choosing a navy dress with a white collar and brass buttons. Mike had planned to join her, and her parents were having a reception for little Jessie. Savannah had already provided the caseworker with a dress for Jessie, and when she picked the baby up, she thought she was the most beautiful little girl she had ever seen.

Mike stood to one side, holding the carrier while the caseworker placed Jessie in Savannah's arms. Jessie smelled of talcum and lotion, and cooed as if she was happy with the arrangement, too. Her big blue eyes gazed up at Savannah, and Savannah's heart melted.

The pink dress with its smocking was pretty on the baby, and her rosy cheeks and rosebud mouth simply added to her sweet beauty. Savannah hugged her, thinking this was one of the most wonderful moments in her life. She looked up to find Mike watching her solemnly.

"Shall we go?" he asked, and she nodded, thanking the state officials and the caseworker and hurrying outside with Jessie.

She kissed Jessie's head, and then in the car, kneeling in the front seat, she fastened a pink bow in Jessie's thin curls.

"My baby, Mike," Savannah told him, while on her knees in the front seat of his new car as he turned on the ignition. "She is so precious, and it's a miracle she's mine." Savannah slid her arms around him and hugged him.

"Hey," he said, switching off the engine and pulling her into his arms so that he cradled her against him.

She laughed and pushed away to sit up. "I'm just grateful."

"Come back here and show me."

"Showing you my gratitude for Jessie isn't what you have in mind. Let's go to my folks'. Everyone is waiting."

When she and Mike arrived, he lifted Jessie out of her carrier and handed her to Savannah.

"Go let your family drool over her and hold her," Mike said, and she wrinkled her nose at him.

"Just wait until *your* family comes. They'll be the same way."

"I'll have to see that to believe it," he said before she hurried away. The rest of the day, everyone hovered over Jessie, taking turns playing with her, feeding her and holding her.

After Jessie was in bed, Mike and Savannah drove out to move some of their things to the inherited house. They toured the huge mansion, looking at an upstairs family room and a downstairs family room, a sunroom, multiple bedrooms, a games room, an exercise room, bathrooms, an enormous dining room, a huge kitchen and the yard with its Olympic-size swimming pool.

"You said this wasn't your style," she reminded him. "It isn't my style, either. I think we're going to get lost in here."

"Maybe we can rent out rooms," he said, and she laughed. He had draped his arm casually around her shoulders and she hadn't moved away.

Savannah's thoughts jumped back to the present, and she glanced at the empty bed, feeling forlorn. This was probably the only wedding night she would ever have, and she was spending it alone. After a few minutes she thought of Jessie, and her spirits lifted.

Savannah fell asleep in the chair and awoke to knocking and someone calling her name.

Six

Savannah shouted, "Wait a minute!"

Running to get her robe, she recognized Mike's voice as he called, "Savannah, are you all right?"

She opened the door a crack to peer up at him. He looked handsome and clean-shaven, his hair slightly damp from a shower. He was dressed in jeans and a short-sleeve navy knit shirt.

"Can I come in? I thought something had happened to you. I was about to pick the lock." Mike pushed slightly, and she stepped back. Standing there in her clingy silk pajamas, she looked sleepy and disheveled. Gone was the cool, collected attorney. Her blond hair was tousled, spilling around her face.

She turned away, but he caught her arm.

"Savannah," he said in a voice that had grown husky, "I woke you, didn't I?"

His dark gaze was riveting as he drew her to him. She slipped out of his grasp and stepped back. "You wait right

here while I get dressed,'' she said breathlessly, warming
when his gaze roamed over her, stirring her raw nerves as
much as if he had trailed his fingers over her instead.

She rushed from the room and closed the bedroom door,
looking at herself in the mirror across the room. The pajama
shirt wasn't even buttoned as high as it should have been.
Her hair was a tangle and a minute ago she had been all
but drooling over him. Swiftly, she showered and dressed
in jeans and a plaid shirt, combing her hair and jamming
her feet into loafers.

''I'm sorry you had to wait. I overslept,'' she said when
she joined him. He looked amused.

Over breakfast she knew he was pouring on the charm.
He told her stories from his childhood, stories about his
brothers. Then it was time to go to the airport and return
home.

The minute they reached Stallion Pass and her parents'
house, they were kept busy. They stayed to eat sandwiches
and then loaded the car with Jessie's things. Mike fastened
Jessie's carrier into the back seat of the new car he had
bought when he moved to Texas.

When they entered the house, Savannah brought Jessie in
her carrier while Mike brought suitcases. At the head of the
stairs, she turned to him. ''Well, take your pick of bedrooms. The only one taken is Jessie's, and I don't think
you'd want all that pink.''

''You take the master bedroom. I don't need or want that
much room,'' Mike told her.

''And it'll be easier when you move out later,'' she added
and got a nod from him that annoyed her. His smug cer-
tainty that he would be able to walk away without any emotional ties to the baby—or to her—was a constant source of
irritation, although Savannah knew she shouldn't let it be.
He had always been clear about his intentions. She headed
toward the large master bedroom. It had an adjoining bath
as big as her condo's living room.

"No wonder they kidnapped him and held him for ransom," Mike breathed, looking at the luxurious bedroom.

"His captors didn't know or care about his house."

"You're right. They knew he was the CEO of an American oil company. That was enough." Mike set down her suitcases. "I'll unpack the car and you take care of the baby."

She nodded and wondered which bedroom he was taking. She'd expected him to get an apartment in San Antonio, which he said he would do sometime in the future, but for now he intended to stay here. Probably with intentions of seducing her, she thought, remembering the previous night.

As she was bringing a bottle back upstairs to Jessie, she saw Mike carrying a box and suitcase into the bedroom next to hers and directly across the hall from Jessie.

She held the baby on her shoulder while she went to the door to watch Mike open his suitcase, which sat on the four-poster bed. "This is where you're staying?" she asked. The room suited him, she thought, with its bare hardwood floor, navy bedspread and heavy mahogany furniture.

"Yes. Does it meet with your approval?"

"Of course. I'm surprised that you're staying in this end of the house. I thought you'd want to be as far away from me as possible."

He put down folded shirts and crossed to her, making her pulse jump. He stood only inches away, his hand against the doorjamb. "The last thing I want to do is be far away from you," he said in a honeyed, seductive voice. He ran a finger down her cheek. "I want you close. In my arms close, and if you weren't holding a baby, I'd show you just how much I want you."

"I am holding her, and she's hungry," Savannah whispered.

"I'll show you later," he said quietly. She sighed, turned and went to Jessie's nursery to feed her.

The evening rushed by as Savannah took care of Jessie,

while Mike moved all their things into the house. The new house staff would arrive the next day, but for tonight, she and Mike were alone with the baby.

Savannah changed into a T-shirt and cutoffs, then went downstairs. Mike was working to put together a baby swing.

He was leaning over the frame, muscles flexing as he worked, and for a moment, Savannah stood and watched him, enjoying the memory of how it had felt to be pressed against his lean, hard body. Shaking her head as if to clear it, she crossed the room.

"I can't stop looking at her because she's such a miracle in my life," Savannah said, carrying Jessie over to Mike. "Hold her while I get a bottle."

She put Jessie in his arms as he sat back cross-legged on the floor. Before Savannah reached the door, Jessie began to cry.

"Come back here, Savannah," Mike said. "She's unhappy."

"Put her on your shoulder."

"You come get her," he said, standing and crossing the room to hand the baby back to her.

Savannah took Jessie, talking softly to the baby as she carried her to the kitchen, where she had a baby seat for Jessie. She put Jessie in the seat and mixed formula, then filled bottles and put them into the refrigerator while she talked to the baby.

"You're going to have to let…" She wasn't sure what to call Mike, realizing that he might be Jessie's legal guardian, but that was all. Savannah shrugged. By the time Jessie could talk much, Mike would be gone.

"You have to let Colonel Remington hold you, sweetie. He's going to be with us for a while." She turned to get a spoon and saw Mike standing in the doorway watching her. He leaned against the jamb, one hand splayed on his hip and his eyebrow cocked.

"'Daddy' might be too much when she starts talking, but

Colonel Remington? Isn't that a little formal for the man who's her guardian and soon will adopt her?"

"Maybe, but Daddy doesn't fit," she said, annoyed with him again and his lack of interest in Jessie. "I don't know why I expected you to fall in love with her, but I did. I thought once you were around her, you wouldn't be able to resist."

"It isn't the baby I can't resist," he said quietly.

She shot him a glance, responding to his words, yet still annoyed. "She's a beautiful little girl, aren't you, sweetie?" Savannah asked, leaning over Jessie, who was bouncing in the baby seat. Savannah smacked her lips and held up a towel to play peek-a-boo with Jessie. In seconds, the little girl was laughing every time Savannah popped out from behind the towel.

Mike watched Savannah. She was going to be a good mother, and she already loved Jessie as if she were her own daughter. As the lady lawyer leaned closer to Jessie, Mike's gaze drifted over her.

The cutoffs were short, tight across Savannah's trim backside, cut high to reveal long, smooth legs. She had caught her hair up on her head in a butterfly clip, and strands of it fell around her face. Desire ignited, and he longed to cross the room and take her into his arms, but he knew he couldn't. She was giving her total attention to Jessie, and he knew he'd annoyed her when he'd handed the baby back to her.

Unable to stay away from Savannah, he crossed the room. "If you'll tell me what to do, I'll finish fixing the bottles. You can play with her while I do this."

"Follow the directions on the can of formula mix," she said abruptly.

While Mike turned to do what she instructed, he heard her talking to Jessie as she picked her up in her little chair and carried her out of the room.

When he had agreed to this marriage, he had planned to

get an apartment in San Antonio and rarely show up at the Stallion Pass house. He hadn't planned to commute between his new office and the Frates mansion. But he found he wanted to be with Savannah, so he'd put off looking for an apartment, telling himself he would do that in a week or two. Yet she had been busy every minute tonight with Jessie, so he might as well have stayed in town for all the chance he got to be alone with her. True, eventually Jessie would be put to bed, but Mike had a feeling Savannah was annoyed with him and it would take him the rest of the night to mend fences with her.

He couldn't stop thinking about last night, how Savannah had looked and felt in his arms. He wanted to hold and kiss her all night, and it was worth putting off an apartment and hanging around the mansion to get to be with her, even though she was busy with the baby.

It was another hour before Savannah rocked Jessie to sleep and carried her to bed. Mike trailed after her, watching her put the baby in her crib as she whispered to her and brushed a kiss across her cheek. She continued to gaze at the sleeping child.

"Are you going to watch her all night?" he asked quietly in the shadows of the darkened room.

"Maybe," she said, glancing at him as if she hadn't realized he was in the room with her. "She's a miracle in my life. She's so beautiful."

"Why do I think you would react that way even if they had given you the plainest baby in the world?"

Savannah walked out of the room, and he turned to fall into step beside her. "I can't believe that I'm going to get to adopt her and raise her. I promise I will never let her forget her real parents."

"Blood parents," he corrected. "You're going to be the real parent."

"You really aren't interested, are you."

"I don't think I was meant for babies and fatherhood and

all that. I told you, a baby doesn't fit into my life. And I can't turn on feelings for her by holding her or watching her.''

''I don't know how you can resist her.'' Savannah sighed. ''Thanks for carrying all my boxes in. I need to start unpacking now.''

He stopped her. ''Let's go sit and have a glass of soda before you do. You're taking tomorrow off work, anyway, to get moved in.''

Together they went to the upstairs family room, which ran across the front of the mansion. Its polished wood floor shone, the boards creaking slightly as they crossed the room to an oversize brown-leather sofa. Savannah sat in a corner and folded her legs beneath her, and Mike sat close enough to rest his arm across the back of the sofa and tangle his fingers in her hair.

''Are you going apartment shopping tomorrow?'' she asked.

''I'll give this a try for a while. It's more interesting here.''

She arched her brows. ''I know it's not Jessie or the house or the town that's drawing you.''

''You know damn well why I'm staying,'' he said, letting his fingers trail to her nape.

''We're not going to have any seduction scene, so if that's why you're hanging around, you may as well move on,'' she said. But her voice had changed, and he knew from touching her that he was affecting her.

''We'd have a lot more pleasure this year.''

''We might. But I've been abandoned twice in my life. I don't want it to happen a third time,'' she said lightly, but she knew that was her deepest fear.

''Haven't you ever had a serious relationship with a man?'' he asked.

''I thought I was in love in college.''

''And when it ended?'' Before she could answer, he tilted

his head to study her. "You're the one who walked, weren't you."

"Yes, when I realized we weren't well suited."

"I don't think there's any danger of us falling in love, then," he said, moving closer and brushing her ear with a kiss.

Savannah pushed against his chest. "I agree with you there. We have a chemistry when we're together—why that is, I can't imagine—but there's no danger of falling in love."

"So why not enjoy each other?"

She gave him an exasperated look. "I've told you—and I know you understand it. Remember, I don't want an emotional entanglement even if we don't fall deeply in love. And if there is physical intimacy, then I *will* have an emotional entanglement. I can't leave my feelings at the door." Savannah's words slowed as she talked. She meant every word she said, but she was far too conscious of his fingers caressing her nape, of his eyes gazing at her hungrily and his lips taunting her as he brushed her ear with kisses. He'd set his drink on the coffee table and now he put hers there.

She knew she should stop him, but the torment was delicious, impossible to resist as he leaned close to trail kisses along her throat. His thick black hair was as irresistible as the rest of him, and she wound her fingers into it, letting short strands slide through her fingers. She closed her eyes, and then his mouth covered hers and his arm slipped around her waist to draw her closer.

Dimly, over her roaring blood, Savannah thought she heard a baby crying. She pushed against Mike and when he raised his head, she listened. "It's Jessie," Savannah said, standing and rushing from the room, wondering how long she could live under the same roof with Mike before she succumbed to his persuasive touch and ended up in his bed. He had made it clear those were his intentions. No pretense there. They had only been married a day, and she was having trouble keeping up her resistance.

She picked up Jessie, who was indeed crying, and held her close. Jessie stopped crying and snuggled in Savannah's arms.

"What's the matter?" Mike asked from the doorway.

"I think all she wants is to be held," Savannah said, crossing the room to him. "After all, she's spent almost four days at my parents' home, where someone held her all the time. I'll rock her back to sleep."

He nodded and left, while Savannah sat in the rocker and sang softly to Jessie as she went back to sleep.

Helga Aldrin, the middle-aged woman who had cooked for the Frateses, returned to cook for Savannah and Mike. The rest of the staff returned, as well—Francois Vernon to take care of the yard, Millie Hasso to clean. The new addition was Constance McGrath, the nineteen-year-old nanny who replaced Jessie's former nanny, who had just recently married and moved away. Taking night classes at Trinity in San Antonio, Constance would stay every day, coming at seven o'clock in the morning and leaving at six o'clock in the evening.

From the first day he opened, Mike was surprised at the business that his new security company received. Then he realized that the Clays had a lot of influence in the area. Consequently, he wasn't going to have to struggle to get clients.

Which he told Savannah when they were alone late Wednesday night. They played pool in the third-floor games room, with two wins for Mike and one for Savannah. Savannah had changed to cutoffs and a T-shirt, and had pinned her hair on her head.

"You're good, Counselor," he said when she won a second game.

She smiled at him. "I've had lots of practice. My brothers like this."

"And you're very competitive. No allowing me to win here."

"You're too good for someone to have to throw a game. And you're right. If you were playing for the first time, I'd still try to beat you. Since it's you, I enjoy winning. Besides, it helps me forget work." She met his gaze across the table.

"Big case?"

"Yes," she said, wanting to put work out of mind. "Let's play one more, then one of us will have the best three out of five."

"Sure thing."

Savannah watched Mike as he moved around the table. His white T-shirt molded to his muscular body. His jeans were tight, low on his narrow hips, and desire coiled inside her. She watched him sink three balls into pockets, then he straightened to look at her.

"How busy are you with your new business?" she asked.

"Thanks to you, I've got several jobs. I may have to hire some people to help me."

"Why 'thanks to me'?"

"People around here and San Antonio like you and your family, and now I'm part of the family. As a matter of fact…" He paused to sink a ball into a pocket. He then walked around the table to take another shot. "I was hired today for something I never thought I'd do. Someone stole your friend Wyatt Sawyer's white stallion. He wants the horse back."

"Why would they steal that horse? The bloodlines can't be good," Savannah said, mystified. "Originally, Gabe Brant caught the stallion and couldn't gentle him, so he gave the horse to Josh, who gave the stallion to Wyatt."

"Well, someone stole that horse and two others of Wyatt's, and he's not happy. I think it's the principle of the thing. He's hired me to catch the horse thief. Shades of the Old West.''

"Livestock and equipment still get stolen in this age. I'm surprised you took the job. A horse thief may be hard to find. People usually write off the loss. Especially when it isn't a high-dollar animal.''

"I think Wyatt is burned that someone did this to him. He doesn't want the thief to get away with it. Wyatt could buy another horse for what it will probably cost him to catch the thief, but that isn't what's worrying him.''

"Well, if anyone can do it, I'm sure you can.''

Mike had circled the table, and now she stood only a couple of feet away. He turned to her, taking her chin in his hand and tilting her face up. ''I didn't know you had that much faith in me.''

"Of course I do,'' she said, looking up into smoldering brown eyes that caused her to think only halfway about what she was saying. ''I married you, didn't I? I wanted you to take charge of Jessie. I read your background. It's impressive.''

He placed his cue stick on the table and took hers from her, and Savannah's pulse raced. Every night they kissed, and each time increased her hunger for him.

"On the other hand, I still know damn little about you. There are some things I particularly want to know. I want to know if I can kiss you into agreeing to do what I want. I want to know what happens when you let go,'' he said. ''I want to know every inch of you—''

He broke off as his mouth covered hers. She slipped her arms around his neck and held him, returning his kisses wildly, knowing she was speeding toward disaster, yet unable to stop.

Mike tugged her T-shirt out of her cutoffs, his hands sliding over her and then cupping her breasts. As his thumbs played across her nipples, she trembled, longing shaking her while she returned his kiss. She slipped her hands beneath his T-shirt and ran her fingers down his smooth back.

Pausing, she gazed up at him. ''I'm not going to let you break my heart.''

''The last thing on earth I'd want to do is hurt you,'' he said, kissing her temple, trailing kisses to her ear.

She caught his face in her hands, forcing him to look at her. ''Did it ever occur to you that after a year here, you might not want to leave? You're running risks, too.''

''I'll leave. I'm not good daddy or family material. I don't know anything about babies.''

''You can learn,'' she said, gazing at him and feeling the same clash of irritation and desire she'd had the first day she met him.

''No, make no mistake, Savannah. I'll live by what we agreed, and when the year is up, I'm gone.''

''Let's go back to our game,'' she said, her breathing still faster than usual. She wanted to step right back into his arms, but instead she wriggled away from him. He looked amused and confident, as if he knew the effect he had on her and knew it was only a matter of time until she was in his bed.

''My family is getting together Saturday to ride. We do this about twice a month. Would you like to join us?'' she asked.

''Sure,'' he answered as he leaned over the table to line up a shot.

''Since your parents once had a ranch in Montana, I assume you ride.''

''Yep. I haven't in a long time, but I did as a kid.''

She fell silent as she watched him, and then concentrated on her game. What was it between them that made her feel so competitive? Whatever it was, it was mutual.

She shook her head in disgust. ''You win,'' she said, putting away her cue stick.

He came around to put his in the rack and then draped his hands on her shoulders. "To the victor go the spoils."

"Not on your nellie," she said.

"You're a sore loser, Counselor. If pool does this to you, I'd hate to see you lose a case."

"I don't lose very often."

"Let's go get a cold drink and sit and talk," he said, lacing his fingers through hers.

"Mike, I think I might like to hire you."

"Oh, darlin', I'm all yours," he said playfully, turning to take her into his arms.

She had to laugh as she pushed against his chest. "To investigate what's happening at my office," she said as he released her.

"That smile has probably done more to win trials for you than all your brilliant arguments," he said.

"Don't be ridiculous, but I'm glad you like my smile."

"Oh, yes, I like your smile, your mouth…" he whispered into her ear, blowing lightly and stirring tingles in her.

"Stop flirting with me!" Savannah said, but she smiled at him.

"I like to flirt with you and see where it leads."

"It's not leading anywhere tonight. And I want to talk to you about my problems at work."

"All right, back to your office."

"In the past few months, we've lost three clients we've had a long time. If it was only one or two, I'd say that was normal. Things always change. But this is three coming very close together."

"What reasons do they give you?"

"One wants a larger firm. One didn't want to pay as much as we charge, but we charge a pretty standard rate."

"I'll be glad to look into it. I'll call tomorrow and set an appointment when I can come to your office. Do you have Troy's approval for this?"

"I don't need it, but I'm sure he would approve, although he doesn't agree with me about why they left."

"I had the feeling at our wedding that he wasn't fond of me."

"Troy can be jealous and a little vindictive, and at our wedding, he thought you and I were in love. I think he was piqued—a damaged male ego. Since then, I've told him the truth. Now he should be friendly."

"We'll see."

They went to the family room to talk. Each night during the week, after Jessie was asleep, Savannah and Mike talked until the wee hours. And each night they kissed, and Savannah knew that with every hour that passed, she wanted him more than she did the hour before.

On Friday morning, Mike came through the door of Savannah's office and her breath caught. She remembered that first day and how her pulse had leaped the moment she'd seen him. And the sparks that ignited that day still had her heart pumping wildly. Today he again wore a navy suit and dark tie, and instantly, she was aware of herself as his dark eyes roamed over her.

"You're smiling," he commented. "Is it in recollection or in satisfaction that you got what you wanted—little Jessie, me, the whole bit?"

"I don't have you, but I do have Jessie. And I'm smiling because I remember the chemistry we both felt and too often still feel. Have a seat."

"Sure thing, Counselor," he said, looking amused.

"You're remembering, too," she said, wanting to pat her hair and make sure it was in place, but resisting the impulse. She wore a navy tailored dress that had a V neckline and brass buttons, and now she wished she'd worn something softer, more feminine and appealing.

"What would you like to know, Mike? I have a list of

the clients we've lost and as much information about them as I could provide," she said, handing a list to him.

A knock at the door interrupted her, and Troy Slocum walked in.

"Mike, you remember meeting my partner, Troy Slocum," Savannah said.

Mike came to his feet and shook hands with the tall blond man, who gazed coldly back at him. "It's nice to see you again," Mike said politely, curious about the animosity he saw in Slocum's eyes.

As Mike sat down again, Troy dropped into another chair and smoothed his gray suit pants over his knees. He turned to Mike. "I told Savannah that this is a waste of your time. Clients leave firms every day. I really don't know what she expects to find."

"You and I have been over this, Troy," Savannah said before Mike could answer. "I think we've lost too many for it to be coincidence. Let's see what Mike can find out about them."

"If it makes you happy, but I think it's a waste of time and money. All he's going to learn is that the companies just wanted a change, maybe in some cases because someone in the company thought they should try another firm. There will probably be as many reasons as there are companies that you're looking into, but if it keeps you busy and Savannah happy, so be it. It's a bone your new wife can toss you."

"Troy, I'm not tossing him a bone. Stop grousing over the expense. Humor me on this one. I have a funny feeling about it."

"Savannah and her feelings. Savannah, we've lost clients before, and then they've come back to us. Look at the Marsden Ltd. group. Or V. R. Hunsacker and Associates. They left. They came back. That'll probably happen with some of these latest clients."

"It might, but I still want Mike to look into it," Savannah said.

"Well," Troy returned, "if I can be of any help to you, Mike, please let me know. I'll do what I can."

"Thanks," Mike replied.

"I've tried, and as much influence as I have on Savannah, I couldn't change her mind on this one."

"Want to go to lunch?" Mike asked Savannah as soon as Troy had closed the door behind him.

"Sure. Let me check on a couple of things and then I'll be ready." She left her office.

Mike looked at Savannah's list of clients. He had a place to begin and it shouldn't take long to get some of the information he needed. He half suspected that Troy was right—companies did like change and her clients could have decided to move on. It could be all coincidental. But he would look into it because it would be quick and easy and would satisfy Savannah.

The next day, they joined her family at her parents' two-story house.

The Clays gathered in the family room, ready to ride once everyone had arrived. When the last brother appeared, they all headed toward the kitchen to go outside to the waiting horses.

Savannah's father was showing Mike a hunting bow he had made, and they lingered after the others had gone. "You better catch up with them," Matt said at last. "This family will only wait so long. You enjoy your ride today. Amy and I will enjoy staying here and watching Jessie and the other kids."

"Yes, sir," Mike answered. When he stepped into the hall, he saw Savannah talking to her brother, Andy. He hurried toward them, but they disappeared into the kitchen. When he was just outside the doorway, he heard them say his name.

"Give Mike Bluebonnet," Andy said.

"I'm doing no such thing. You two just want to see him bucked off. He gets Jester."

"Aw, give him Bluebonnet, Savannah. He's tough." Mike recognized Lucius's voice.

"You ride your horse and I'll ride my horse and we'll give Mike Jester. End of discussion."

When Mike entered the kitchen, the subject was instantly changed.

"We're ready," Lucius said, his eyes twinkling. "The horses are saddled and ready to go."

As they walked to the waiting horses, Mike put his arm around Savannah's shoulders and pulled her close.

"How long since you've ridden?" she asked.

"A very long time."

"You take Jester and you'll be fine."

"I wasn't worried about it." Savannah smiled at him and turned to wave to her folks, who stood on the back steps holding Jessie, while half-a-dozen grandchildren played in the yard.

When they reached the horses, the men mounted. "Mike, take Bluebonnet over there," Lucius said.

"No, take Jester," Savannah countered, grabbing the reins of a big bay gelding and leading it back to Mike. While Mike took the reins from her and swung into the saddle, the men and their wives headed out.

Mike urged Jester into a walk as Savannah mounted her sorrel mare.

The late-April sunshine was warm, and Mike suspected that by noon it would be sweltering, but the ride would be over by then and they'd all be ensconced in the air-conditioned house.

Mike noticed that the others had stopped, waiting for him and Savannah to catch up.

"Mike!" Savannah's father came charging across the backyard.

At the same time, Mike felt Jester tense, and then the horse exploded into the air and landed stiff-legged to leap up again as if he had springs for legs.

Mike tightened his legs and gritted his teeth, aware of Savannah's father yelling and her brothers and Savannah doubled over with laughter.

Mike didn't know how long he could hang on, but he was determined to stick like a burr. The wild laughter changed to shouts of encouragement.

"Ride 'em cowboy!" Cheers went up from her brothers until finally Jester stopped bucking and was still, snorting and pawing the earth. Applause went up from the onlookers, and Savannah's father stood nearby with his hands on his hips. He shook his head in disgust and turned to head back to the house.

The others rode away while Savannah urged her mount forward toward Mike. Her eyes sparkled and a smile hovered on her lips. "You've kept your talents hidden. You must have done the rodeo circuit. My brothers were impressed."

"You wanted to see me land on my rear and get a mouthful of dirt."

"No!" she answered with wide-eyed innocence. "I knew you'd be able to ride Jester."

Mike looked past her. The riders were disappearing beyond a grove of trees. He swung out of the saddle and looped the reins around the nearby fence, then reached out to take the reins to her horse. "Get down, Savannah."

Seven

"**O**h, no! Don't tell me you're a sore loser."

He reached up and lifted her off her horse, standing her on her feet in front of him. She knew she had played an ornery trick on him, but that tension was still there between them, and an urge to get the best of him plagued her constantly. Instead, he had ridden Jester like a pro, and now the fire in his eyes made her heart lurch.

They stood between the two horses, blocked from the view of the other riders and the house.

"I could've broken my neck," he said in a tone that made her realize he wasn't angry at all. Her trick had had the opposite effect. His dark eyes were filled with passion, and she didn't know if it was from the adrenaline rush he'd just had or if he was determined to get back at her in a way that suited him.

"Not true," she protested swiftly. "You grew up on a ranch. I knew you'd know how to ride."

"You're not talking your way out of this one, darlin'," he drawled.

"Mike—"

"Play with fire and you know what happens. After that little trick you played on me, I deserve to get what I want this morning." He pulled her close and his mouth came down hard on hers in a kiss that took her breath and made her heart pound violently.

His tongue touched and stroked and taunted, stirring desire into white heat, causing her to tremble in his arms and forget where they were or what had happened.

Consumed by his kiss and aching for more, she pressed against him and wrapped her arms around his neck. While she wound her fingers in his hair, her world tipped crazily.

Finally he released her, and they stood staring at each other, gasping for breath. "I'll finish what I've started when we're home tonight," he said in a husky voice that strummed her raw nerves.

They continued to look at each other as if both were reluctant to end the spell woven by his kiss. She wanted to fling herself back into his arms, and she knew he felt the same way.

He caught her chin in his fingers. "You and I are like fire and dynamite—a volatile combination. I ought to be angry, but all I want to do is kiss you until all that fire in you is mine."

"Well, I didn't get the reaction from you I expected," she said, barely aware of her words because her pulse still thrummed and she tingled from head to toe, wanting him and knowing she had stirred up a world of trouble with her prank.

"There's another horse saddled for you to ride," she said. She caught the reins of both horses to lead them back to the corral. A black horse stood saddled and waiting, and Savannah motioned toward it. "There's your horse."

"So what's this one going to do? Another bucking contest?"

"Believe me, the pranks are over. He's docile."

Mike looked amused as he swung into the saddle and urged his horse beside hers, but Savannah was in a turmoil now, too conscious of his promise to continue when they were home alone tonight what he had started with his passionate kiss.

"My brothers will be so impressed with you. They'll be nicer to you now."

"You and your brothers set me up this morning with that talk about which horse I should ride. You knew I'd overhear you."

"Sorry, Mike. I couldn't resist trying to shake you up a bit."

"And I intend to shake you up in return. You asked for it, Savannah," he said in a voice like a caress.

Later, as Mike rode behind her, he watched her trim derriere and thought about the morning's kiss. He intended to keep his promise to her. She had pushed him this morning, and he was going to push back tonight. Only it wasn't exactly pushes between them, but rather a simmering clash that had desire as its bedrock.

When they had caught up with her family, all of them congratulated him on staying on Jester's back. To Mike's amusement, some of the animosity he had sensed around her brothers was gone.

"Good job. I'll take you to lunch one day this week," her youngest brother, Jacob, said. "We had a bet on whether you'd stick on Jester or not, and I won, so you get a free lunch."

"Thanks, give me a call," Mike answered easily, giving Savannah a look.

Back home, Savannah's father gave her a lecture, then

turned to Mike to congratulate him on his ride. Here, too, Mike sensed a thawing of her father's attitude toward him, although he knew the thawing had started when he had danced with Savannah at the wedding reception and they had looked like two people in love.

Maybe her family thought he would fall in love with her and stay. Fortunately, at least Savannah didn't expect that. He watched her as they packed the car to go home, thinking she seemed too earnest about life to be into practical jokes. He suspected she would think twice before involving him in another one.

It was almost ten o'clock that night before she put Jessie down. As soon as she did, she called to Mike, who was in the family room.

"Good night, Mike. It's been a long day, and I'll see you in the morning."

He heard her bedroom door close. It was clear she was avoiding being alone with him, but he wouldn't forget what he had said this morning. His time would come. If not tonight, then soon. Very soon...

The next few days were too busy for Savannah and Mike to have any moments with only the two of them.

Friday afternoon, his cell phone rang as he was coming out of a client's office. When he answered, he heard Savannah's voice.

"Mike, I need your help."

"What's wrong?" he asked, thinking only Jessie could cause the panic he heard in Savannah's voice.

"Constance's father had a heart attack and she has to leave this afternoon as soon as we can get home to relieve her. I'm tied up here at the courthouse."

"I'll take care of it. I can pick Jessie up and take her to your mom's house or to one of your sisters'."

"No, you can't. The whole family has packed up and

gone to Fort Worth for the horse show, remember? You and I were too busy to join them.''

He didn't remember, but he tried to think of someone else to care for Jessie. Helga was off on Friday afternoons and Millie Hasso, who cleaned the house, wouldn't want to deal with a baby. ''What about one of your friends?''

''I can't get anyone,'' she said.

Panic gripped him. Jessie cried every time he picked her up, and he couldn't imagine caring for her by himself for even an hour. ''Savannah—''

''Please, Mike. Surely you can manage one little baby for a couple of hours.''

''Savannah, this isn't one of your practical jokes, is it?''

''I swear it's not! I need your help desperately and Constance needs to go.''

''Damn. All right, but you get there as fast as you can— and I better not find out this is a joke.''

''Mike, it's not. Will you call Constance and tell her that you're coming? And thanks!'' The phone clicked and Savannah was gone.

He glanced at his watch and lengthened his stride as he moved to his car. He called Constance on his cell and told her he would be there as fast as possible.

As he drove to Stallion Pass, he thought about the things he had planned to do the remainder of the afternoon. As soon as he could, he'd make some calls.

At the house, Constance was standing at the back door. She waited with her purse hooked over her shoulder and her books in her arms.

''Thanks, Mike, for coming so quickly. I'm sorry, but I have to run.''

''I hope your father is all right and gets better quickly.''

''Thanks,'' she said, walking backward as she talked to him. ''Jessie is asleep. There are bottles in the fridge, and baby food is on the counter.''

"Sure. Take all the time you need with your dad."

She nodded as she ran to her car.

Having seen how messy it could be to feed Jessie, Mike changed into jeans and a T-shirt and then sat down to make his calls, praying Jessie slept until Savannah showed up. Of all times for her entire family to go to a horse show! What rotten luck.

Just as he finished his last call, he heard Jessie's wails over the intercom. He hurried to the nursery and found her bawling and kicking. She wore a rumpled red jumper and a white knit shirt. Her brown curls were matted with perspiration and her face matched her jumper.

"Shh, baby," he said, picking her up. She only screamed louder. "I'm sorry, but you've got me today. Let's get you changed and fed." He carried her to the changing table.

It took three diapers and a multitude of tries before he got a diaper on her that looked as if it would stay. By that time her screams and kicks were worse than ever.

"Shh, sweet baby. I'm doing the best I can," he said softly, feeling panicky and wanting to put her in the car and drive to a neighbor's for help, but he didn't know the neighbors. If he had met them at the wedding reception, he didn't remember them.

"Oh, saints preserve us, Savannah, get home!" he muttered to himself. "Dammit, woman, you got me into this!" He changed his tone, trying to talk softly, coax Jessie to stop crying.

He got her a bottle, heated it and held it for her, tucking her into the crook of his arm. She shoved it away, still screeching, and Mike's panic mushroomed. What could he do to calm her? Her face was beet red and she was beginning to gurgle as she cried, and he was scared she would choke.

He could not remember ever feeling so scared, so out of control. He had been more in control when he was under fire from a sniper. At least he could shoot back or try to get away, but he didn't know of anything he could do here.

"Sweet baby," he crooned, singing what he knew of a lullaby he had heard Savannah sing, but Jessie didn't seem to like his singing. He got the bouncy baby chair and set it on the table, then buckled her into it and bounced it, all the while pleading softly with her.

"Please, please, stop crying, sweetie. Please, I'm doing the best I can. I don't know whether something hurts you or you're angry to be stuck with me. But please, Jessie, stop crying."

He opened a jar of applesauce and tried to feed her, but she batted it away angrily and in minutes it was spattered on his shirt, the floor and the table. Mike grabbed a paper towel and mopped up. Okay, so much for trying to feed her solids.

He picked up the newspaper that lay on the table and hid behind it, then popped out and said, "Peek-a-boo!"

To his amazement, her eyes widened and her cries diminished. He tried it again and she hiccupped, then shuddered and took a deep breath. He popped out from behind the paper and she laughed, a big laugh that shook her whole body, and suddenly Mike felt as if he had saved the world.

"Ah, sweetie, you are a doll!" he said, hiding behind the paper and popping out again, getting another big laugh from her. "Golly, I need to get the camera!" he said. "Your mama will never believe this." He gave a silent prayer of thanks that Jessie was happy.

After a couple more peek-a-boos, Mike unbuckled her from the baby chair and picked her up again, offering her the bottle. This time Jessie grabbed it, and he brought her into the family room to rock her.

He settled her in the crook of his arm, tucking a towel under her chin while she sucked happily. Her tiny fingers played over the bottle and he marveled at them, seeing why

Savannah was so fascinated by the baby. She was a beautiful little girl. He touched her tiny hand lightly, and her fingers closed around his index finger. He looked at her to see her watching him.

"You are a sweetie," he said softly.

She smiled at him and then went back to sucking the nipple, and Mike's heart melted. He leaned down to kiss the top of her head.

He rocked and sang softly, holding her on his shoulder to let her burp as he had seen Savannah do and rocking her until she finished her bottle. He spread a blanket on the floor and put some of her toys on it, then sat down to play with her, making her laugh again.

It was after ten o'clock that night before Savannah un-locked the door-and stepped inside. The house was quiet and she called softly, "Mike?"

When she went upstairs, she saw a light spilling through the open door to Jessie's room.

Savannah paused in the doorway. Mike was in the rocker, holding Jessie against his chest. They were both asleep. She wondered how he had gotten along. She put down her things and crossed the room to take Jessie from him. The minute she leaned over him, his eyes opened. Then his hand closed around her arm.

"You're home," he said in a deep, sleep-filled voice.

"Yes, and I didn't mean to wake you. I'll put her in the crib."

"I can do that," he said, and Savannah stepped back as Mike got to his feet and placed Jessie down gently.

"Thanks so much, Mike."

He nodded his head toward the door. "Let's go down the hall where we can talk without waking her."

Savannah picked up her things and moved down the hall beside him, lengthening her stride. In the family room, Mike turned on a small lamp and crossed to the bar. "What would you like to drink?"

"A soda. Anything wet and cold."

"Did you have dinner?

"No, but I don't want any now," she said. "How did you get along?"

"We got along fine," he answered.

"Fine?" Savannah's brows arched. "It doesn't look like it," she said, laughing as she gestured at all the food stains on his shirt.

"We did get along," Mike assured her. "She just didn't want to eat any applesauce when she first woke up."

Mike carried glasses of ice and soda to the sofa and motioned for her to come sit. Savannah kicked off her shoes, shed her suit coat and let her hair down, shaking her head. As she turned, she found Mike watching her with that quiet intensity she found so unnerving.

"You're beautiful, Savannah."

"Thank you." She smiled at him and sat down facing him, folding her legs beneath her. She ran her fingers across her forehead.

"Headache?"

"A little. But it's just this one case. We need to do more research."

He listened, and while she talked he set his drink on the coffee table and took hers from her. "Lie down, and I'll give you a back rub," he said.

"I'd welcome that. Though I may fall asleep during it. I'm exhausted, and I have to go into the office tomorrow to work on the case. I'm meeting Troy at eight in the morning. Do you mind taking care of Jessie one more time?"

"No, I don't," he replied, surprised to realize he looked forward to the idea.

When he stood, Savannah stretched out on the sofa on

her stomach, scooting over so he could sit beside her. He began to massage her shoulders. "You're tense."

"It's been a tense day. You actually got along all right with Jessie?" she asked dubiously.

"Yep, after a hair-raising thirty minutes or so, she decided she liked me."

Savannah turned her head to smile at him. "I'm glad. I knew she'd come around. If you were taking care of me, I wouldn't scream and holler."

She turned her head back and her hair hid her face. Mike pulled strands out of the way and saw that her eyes were closed. He began to massage her back again. He leaned down by her ear. "Someday, I'll know what you'll do when I'm 'taking care of you,'" he said in a husky voice. He moved her hair to trail kisses along her nape.

"What happened to the back rub?" she murmured sleepily, and he sat up to continue rubbing her back. In minutes she was breathing evenly and had fallen asleep.

Mike covered her with a light blanket, pausing to look down at her. Desire smoldered in him and he wanted to carry her to bed, but he knew she was exhausted and might have another trying day tomorrow. He left the room, switching off the lamp as he went.

Savannah stirred, coming awake. She sat up disoriented, and then remembered Mike's giving her a massage. A glance at her watch showed it was almost one o'clock in the morning. Moving to her room, she was too tired to change, so she pulled off her jewelry, her panty hose and skirt, falling into bed in her undies, her half-slip and her silk blouse.

It seemed only minutes before Savannah was wakened again, this time by Jessie's loud cries. Concerned that the baby had been crying a long time, Savannah raced to the nursery and picked Jessie up. In minutes she had her quiet and changed, and she carried the baby to the kitchen to get a bottle.

Only the light over the stove was on, but it was sufficient to see. As she got a bottle and warmed it in the microwave, Mike came in the door.

She gasped in surprise. "You startled me," she said, eyeing him and realizing he had come in from outside. He was dressed in jeans, a black T-shirt and black boots; a pair of black gloves was tucked into his waistband.

"You've been out?" she asked, frowning.

Eight

He didn't answer for a moment and she realized how intently he was looking at her. Then she became conscious of her lack of clothing.

"Yeah, I've been out," he replied at last, crossing the room to her. Jessie had grabbed the bottle and was busily sucking on it while Savannah held her. Savannah's pulse jumped and she couldn't take her eyes off Mike.

"Where on earth have you been?" she asked, knowing he didn't have to answer to her about his whereabouts at night or any other time. "I didn't expect to see you," she said breathlessly. "You never wake up when Jessie cries."

She realized the top three buttons to her silk blouse were unfastened, and she reached up to fasten them. Mike's fingers closed over her hand, and her gaze flew up to meet his smoldering dark eyes.

"Leave it, Savannah," he said huskily. He leaned down to trail his tongue along the open V of her blouse.

Tingles radiated from his touch, centering low inside her.

"Mike, I have to feed Jessie," she protested, but her voice was faint.

He straightened to look at her and the desire in his eyes made her heart thud. "Go feed her." He stepped aside and she left him, and it wasn't until she was seated in the rocker in the nursery that she remembered Mike had never answered where he had been.

Now she was wide awake, stirred by his tongue on her bare skin, desire a hot flame that burned away any exhaustion she had experienced earlier.

She fed Jessie, rocked her back to sleep and placed her in her crib, leaning over to kiss her gently. When she turned, she was startled for a second time that evening by Mike, who was leaning against the doorjamb.

"What are you doing in here?" she asked, her pulse racing.

"I wanted to see you when you finished feeding Jessie."

"Let me get my robe," she said, but when she reached the door, Mike's arm shot out, blocking her way. She looked up at him.

"I seem to remember some unfinished business..."

"It's the middle of the night."

"Doesn't matter," he said quietly, wrapping his arms around her and covering her mouth with his.

"Mike," she twisted away to protest, but his mouth covered hers again and she went up in flames. Her arms wrapped around his neck, and she felt as if all the hunger and passion and desire that had been building in him had been poured into his kiss. His tongue played with hers, stroking, thrusting with an insistence that shook her. Hunger for him mushroomed, escalating beyond anything she had ever imagined.

He walked her backward through the open door into her room, then he kicked the door shut behind them.

His fingers twisted loose the pearl buttons on her silk blouse, and he shoved the blouse off her shoulders. While her heart drummed in anticipation, her blouse fell with a soft whisper around her ankles. Mike leaned back to yank off his black T-shirt and toss it aside. With a deft flick of his wrist, he unfastened the clasp of her bra and pushed it away.

Frustration and longing destroyed caution. Every night she dreamed of Mike, longed for him every day and tingled with every physical contact. She wanted his kisses and caresses. She wanted to touch and kiss him, and she yearned to reach him on a deeper level to create more than the casual bonding they shared now.

Savannah ran her hands over his smooth, sculpted chest. As she did, he cupped her breasts in his large tanned hands, and she could hear the sharp intake of his breath. His thumbs drew lazy circles on her nipples.

Savannah gasped at the sensations bombarding her. She grasped his upper arms, clinging as she trembled with a need that threatened to consume her.

"Mike, please..." she whispered.

"Please what? Do you want this?" he said, leaning down to take her nipple in his mouth and circle the taut bud with his tongue.

She moaned, throwing back her head, drowning in desire that raged like a bonfire.

"Or do you want this, Savannah?" He tugged up her half-slip with one hand while his other arm held her around the waist. His fingers brushed her lightly between the legs, and she cried out, arching her hips toward him, unable to resist him.

She clung to him as if he were the only solid thing in a world spinning out of control.

"Answer me," he insisted in a lazy murmur. "What do you like? Do you like my hand here?" His fingers slid inside her panties to stroke her intimately.

She gasped, her back arching while she moaned softly. She wanted him with an intensity she had never known before. If she didn't want heartbreak, however, he was as forbidden to her as owning the moon. She ran her hands across his broad shoulders, down over his flat, muscled stomach. She opened her eyes to see mirrored in his the desire she felt. Kissing him passionately, she wanted to devour him. She wanted to give herself completely to him, even knowing that would be disaster.

Through his jeans, she could feel his thick hard shaft against her, and she couldn't resist moving her hips, pressing against him as closely as she could.

Winding her fingers in his hair, her heart thudding, she fought an inner battle to stop succumbing to his seduction before she was hopelessly lost.

He shifted slightly, his hand trailing down, caressing her breast, her nipple, his fingers trailing lower over her hip, pushing away the half-slip.

She caught his wrist. "Mike," she gasped, "wait. You're going too fast for me."

"This isn't too fast, Savannah. You want this," he said, his fingers sliding beneath her panties to stroke her intimately. "Tell me you don't. Tell me to stop."

She knew she should stop him, but his caresses were storming her logic, sending desire into an all-consuming need. "Mike," she whispered, wanting him.

Knowing that in seconds she would be beyond return, she twisted and caught his arm, opening her eyes to find him watching her with a blazing hunger that was as devastating as his kisses.

"You have to stop! I'm not ready for what you want."

He leaned down to kiss her throat, trailing kisses to her ear to whisper to her, "You tell me to stop, Savannah, and I'll stop, but you don't want to stop. You respond to me beyond my wildest yearnings."

"I know I respond," she gasped. "From that first day, there's been a volatile chemistry between us, but I've told you, I'm not ready for a relationship on your terms."

"We're married," he whispered, kissing her throat, cupping her breasts with his hands, then stroking her nipples in slow, erotic circles that drove her wild. "We're married, compatible, cooperating—why have so much resistance to something we both want and something that could be so fantastic?"

"Because there's too much about you I like," she whispered, catching his face in her hands and feeling the rough stubble on his jaw. "I don't want to fall in love with you, Mike, and then watch you walk out on me later. Delight today doesn't compensate for a world of pain in the future."

"Then let's enjoy each other without falling in love," he whispered as he turned his head and kissed the palm of her hand.

"I'm not ready for that, either," she said, wanting him and wondering if she was throwing away happiness. "I wish I could take a relationship as casually as you do," she said, brushing a kiss across his lips.

He caught her around her waist and pulled her back to kiss her long and passionately before he released her. "I want you, Savannah. I want to love you all night long. I want to know every inch of you. I can wait, but I want you."

The dark promises in the depths of his brown eyes made her want to take what he offered, to move into his world, a world of ecstasy she had never known. And she was certain it would be ecstasy with Mike, but she was equally certain he would abandon her and break her heart. She knew the pain of abandonment and its devastating repercussions too well.

She picked up her bra, holding her arms crossed in front of her. "You need to go."

He touched her cheek lightly. "Someday, you won't tell me to go."

"You're so sure of yourself."

"I'm sure of what you want, too. Good night, darlin'."

He dropped a kiss on her lips, then leaned down to trail his tongue across the tops of her breasts above her crossed arms.

"Mike!" She closed her eyes, aching to step into his arms and love him all night long. Accept the heartache, along with the joy.

When she opened her eyes, he was gone. She was weak, more uncertain than anytime she could remember. She was on fire for him. She crossed the room to close her bedroom door, then switched on a lamp, moving around without thinking about what she was doing, pulling on her silk pajamas. She tingled all over, her nerves raw and an ache low inside that only Mike could banish.

She switched off the light, but then couldn't sleep. She finally got up to sit by the window and look at the shadows on the lawn. And then she remembered Mike coming back into the house dressed all in black. Where had he been in the middle of the night? What had he been doing?

It was almost dawn when she fell asleep, and she overslept, coming awake with a start, listening for Jessie, who usually awakened her on Saturday. Then she remembered he had to go into the office. Savannah tossed aside the sheet and dashed to shower and change, wondering if the baby was sleeping longer than usual.

When Savannah was dressed in dark slacks and a white silk shirt, her hair pinned up, she rushed to the nursery to find it empty.

Surprised that Mike must have picked up Jessie, Savannah hurried downstairs and stopped at the door of the family room. Mike lay stretched on the floor, holding a teddy bear and playing with Jessie, who was buckled into her baby chair.

Mike made growling sounds while he wiggled the bear and then touched Jessie's tummy. "Kiss, kiss," he said, and smacked his lips. The baby giggled.

Savannah's heart turned over, and she knew in that moment she was falling head over heels in love with this man

who would walk out of her life all too soon. Always before
when she'd been drawn to Mike, she'd been stopped shor
by his lack of interest in Jessie.

Staring at him, Savannah knew that her last real defense
against falling for him had just gone out the window. His
hair was tousled, he hadn't shaved, and he was bare-chested
and barefoot.

Riveted, she was unable to tear herself away from watch
ing him with the baby.

"I thought she didn't like you," Savannah said finally.

He glanced at her, his gaze raking over her as he sat up
She waved her hand. "Don't get up," she said. "She's
happy, so you stay right where you are. But since when did
all this come about?"

"Since yesterday," he said, touching the top of Jessie's
head in a loving gesture that pulled at Savannah's heart
strings. "She must have decided I wasn't an ogre, after all,'
he continued, wiggling the teddy bear, "because she and
are chums now, aren't we, li'l sweetie?" he asked, and
gently nuzzled the baby, tickling her neck with his stubbly
chin.

Jessie laughed and put both her hands on his cheeks, hold
ing his face while he made funny noises and whistled. She
laughed some more. He turned to look over his shoulder a
Savannah. "See? Friends." His brows arched and he pulled
away from Jessie to turn and look more closely at Savannah

"You seem less than happy to find out she likes me, afte
all."

"I'm very glad she likes you and vice versa," she said
Savannah's voice was breathless. "If I look unhappy, it'
because as long as you didn't have any interest in her no
Jessie in you, I could resist you. Now it's going to be harde
than ever."

In an easy unfolding, he came to his feet and crossed t
her, tilting up her chin. "I'll tell you what is harder tha
ever—me, with wanting you," he said. "If you didn't have

to be at your office, I'd take down your hair and begin where we left off last night," he said, sliding his arms around her.

Her heart drummed. "Well, you can't. And I do have to go to work."

"But I can kiss you goodbye," he said, and leaned down to kiss her long and thoroughly, igniting fires that had banked in the night and making her want to forget work and the world.

She pushed against his chest and leaned away. "This isn't fair. You're sexy, too appealing. Now you've made little Jessie love you and you care for her—it makes a devastating combo, as you well know."

"I can't see that it's doing me a lot of good," he remarked dryly.

"Unfortunately, it's doing you more good than you can ever begin to realize. You're demolishing my resistance to you and I suspect soon enough, you'll see to what extent. Right now, you know I have to go to work."

"You tell me something like that and then want to walk out as if it's nothing—talk about demolishing someone—" He framed her face with his hands. "You stormed into my life, Savannah, and changed it forever."

They stood only inches apart and he held her head, forcing her to give him her full attention. He couldn't begin to guess the depth of the effect he had on her, but she knew that volatile attraction was increasing enormously today. "I don't see any 'forever' changes in you," she said, barely able to get out the words.

"Then look again. You've made me like taking care of a baby girl—that's a monumental change."

"So you do have a heart after all, Mike. John Frates was so sure of you—I knew you had to be the man he thought you were and not the indifferent person you presented to me at first."

"You've made me change. I want you, Savannah. I want to love you for hours on end. You'll be mine."

"I think I've underestimated you too many times," she said. "But then maybe you've underestimated me, too."

"Never. You've been devastating from that first moment in your office."

She smiled and wriggled out of his grasp. "That's a bunch of rubbish. We clashed—that lion and tiger thing." She stepped away from him.

"I'm late and I need to go now. Are you all right with Jessie, or do I need to do anything before I go?"

He glanced at the baby, who was happily kicking and bouncing in her chair. "We're fine."

She nodded and gave him a long look. "If you have a heart, then you also can love and be loved—and I mean real love, not infatuation," she said.

"Don't imagine qualities that I don't have."

"I wouldn't dream of it," she said with amusement and saw sparks flash in his eyes. As she started to turn, Mike caught her wrist. "When will you be home?"

"I hope by noon, but I may be gone all day."

He nodded and she started to leave, but then turned back to ask, "Where did you go last night all dressed in black?"

"To look for a horse."

"Wyatt's stolen stallion?" she asked in surprise.

"Yep, and I found out where he is. I'll bet we can get him back for Wyatt."

"Where is the horse? Who has him?"

"Right where Wyatt thought he might be. There are some no-goods who live in the county and never liked Wyatt's father, although from what I hear, most folks in the county and the next three never liked Wyatt's father, including Wyatt himself."

Savannah listened and was curious, but she also was unable to keep her gaze from drifting over Mike's bare chest. She realized there was silence, and she looked up into his mocking brown eyes.

She felt her face flush hotly, but tried to remember what

they were talking about. "I better get to work," she said, flustered and embarrassed to be so blatantly undone by the sight of his naked chest. She started out of the room and then remembered they were talking about the missing white stallion.

"How did you find out who has the horse? And how can you be certain it was Wyatt's horse?"

"I saw it in Rory Gandy's pasture, and the stallion has Wyatt's brand."

"A brand barely shows on a white horse," she said.

"I got close. I don't think Gandy is the smartest person in these parts."

"You were on Rory Gandy's land last night?" she asked.

"I didn't get caught. Now don't get your lawyer dander up. I looked in his pasture, saw the horse and left."

"You could have been shot for trespassing."

"Could have been, but wasn't, and now we know where the horse is."

"Are you going to steal him back?" she asked, unhappy with what he'd just admitted.

"Hell no. I'm going to do something legal—get a warrant to search his property and let the law find the horse. All aboveboard and legal."

"So how are you going to do that?"

"Aren't you late for work?"

"You don't want me to know what you're doing. You are going to do something illegal."

"Absolutely not, but since you're a lawyer, I don't think you would approve. I will sort of set Gandy up, whereby he will tip his own hand about the horse and we can get a warrant."

"You're right. I don't want to know, but do you do things like that often? I mean sneaking into places where you could get shot?"

"Nope. That's unique. Worried about my safety, darlin'? Or my scruples?" he asked, grinning.

She glared at him and then had to laugh and shake her head. "Incorrigible man! I'm getting out of here. You've made me late and now I'm worried about you and that job of yours."

"So you do care. That makes my day."

She shook her head and left.

Nine

Savannah didn't get home until nine o'clock that night. She came in the back door, entered the kitchen and stopped in surprise.

Through the glass doors to the patio, she could see that a table was set with place mats and candles in crystal candlesticks. Enticing odors of coffee and warm bread filled the house.

As she stood looking at everything, Mike came through the door. Since she had last seen him, he'd showered and shaved—the ends of his hair were still damp. He wore a knit shirt and jeans, and looked handsome enough to make her weak at the knees.

"You're home," he said unnecessarily.

"I'm impressed. You did this for me?"

"Yes." He opened a bottle of red wine, poured two glasses and brought one to her.

"This is wonderful. Where's Jessie?"

"She's sound asleep, and she went down only ten

minutes ago. Not only that, she had a big meal of oatmeal and applesauce and a full bottle, so she should sleep, hopefully, through the night. We may have the evening to ourselves. We can eat outside and still hear Jessie over the intercom. So how about a swim to unwind?''

"Fabulous! I'm exhausted and this is wonderful, Mike,'' she said again, truly thankful to come home to a prepared dinner and order. "I'm sorry to miss seeing Jessie, but I'll make up for it tomorrow. Before the swim, I'd like to shower. I feel grubby.''

"Want me to come scrub your back?'' he asked softly.

"No!'' she answered with a laugh. "Thanks for the offer. I won't be long.''

She rushed upstairs, feeling giddy and happy and forgetting the case she'd worked on all day. She and Mike had both used the pool, but never at the same time before.

As she showered, she felt a bubbling anticipation for the evening ahead. She slipped into her black, one-piece swimsuit and went downstairs to find Mike already in the pool.

Patio lights gave a golden glow and soft music played. The smell of charcoal and mesquite came from the grill. Blue tiles shone through the crystal-clear water of the pool, and the lights made the pool an iridescent jewel in the darkened patio. Savannah, however, was acutely aware of the virile male in the water.

She made a running dive, slicing the cool water. She came up for a breath and looked around for Mike.

He swam up, his dark eyes twinkling. "Remember Jester? I think this is where I get even.''

"Don't you dare!'' she said, swimming away from him. He caught her, and she struggled with him, clamping her mouth closed before he dunked her. She came bobbing up, sputtering, then hit the surface of the water with the palm of her hand to splash water into his face.

"Mike Remington, you rascal!'' Laughing, she lunged at him, intending to push him under, but he caught her easily and pinned her arms to her sides, his legs tangling with hers. And then she looked into his eyes and saw them change, the twinkle disappearing and desire taking its place.

Her heart hammered as she became aware of their bodies pressed together, her legs entangled with his. He cupped her head with his hand while his other arm banded her waist, holding her tightly against him.

"Savannah," he whispered, his voice filled with longing. He pulled her to him to kiss her, his mouth coming down hard and possessively. She could feel his legs as he kicked slightly, and in minutes her toes touched the bottom of the pool and then they were standing.

Savannah lost track of time or where they were. She was focused on Mike's body pressed against her, his thick shaft hard between them while he kissed her with staggering hunger. All the needs she'd tried to keep banked burst into flame. She ran her hands over his warm, sleek shoulders and then slid her fingers down his bare chest, leaning back away from him slightly.

Mike reached up to the shoulder straps of her suit, peeling them down her arms and baring her breasts. She tingled, quivered under his gaze, wanting his touch and kiss.

"You're beautiful," he said, his voice a hoarse rasp as he leaned down to kiss her, circling one taut nipple with his tongue and causing her to gasp. Electric currents shot through her veins.

He took her nipple into his mouth, sucking lightly, his tongue a sweet torment. She slid her hands down his rib cage, then down over his hips to his muscled thighs.

He peeled her suit farther down, slipped off his own, and then pressed his warm body against her, his hot, hard shaft thrusting. She slid her hand down, her fingers closing around him to stroke him.

He groaned, covering her mouth with his again. He kissed her with such intensity she was turned inside out.

His hands slipped over her wet body, sliding everywhere, stroking, stirring passion, making her want so much more.

She wriggled and slipped out of his grasp, then swam swiftly away from him. But he followed, caught her and placed his hands on her hips.

"I want you to be mine, Savannah. I've wanted you since the first day we met, but the longer I've known you, the more that need has grown." She looked into his dark-brown eyes, her heart pounding at his words. All she could think of was how much she wanted him. How much she wanted him to love her into oblivion. She took his face in her hands.

"You know you can make me melt and you know I want you, Mike, but you know why I'm fighting you. I know a lot about you, but there is a world of knowledge about you that you keep hidden from me. There's something in those dark eyes of yours, something deep in your soul that you don't want to share. Part of you is shut away, and you have no intention of letting anyone else get at it."

Something flickered in his eyes and then they became shuttered. He pulled her to him and kissed her, but she had seen his reaction and knew she was right. And knew she should proceed at her own risk, because he was making no promises.

As soon as she pushed against his chest, he released her. Both of them were breathing hard again, and she stared at him, shaken by the expression on his face. It made her feel wanted beyond measure.

"You're a tough man, Mike. Tough and solitary. You want me to share my body. I want you to share your soul."

"If I did, you might regret it," he said tersely, and turned to swim away, his strong arms slicing through the water.

Something inside her hurt. She wanted him and—against all good judgment—was falling in love with him. She suspected she'd been falling in love with him for some time now, but this morning with Jessie had been the final irresistible stroke.

What was it he kept from everyone? Dark moments from his career? She hadn't found any dark secrets in his child-hood. He seemed close to his brothers and his parents. And then she remembered Colin Garrick's parents and his younger brother, Kevin, and how Mike had tears in his eyes when he'd greeted them. He always said Colin died in the line of duty and that was all he would say, but then he didn't talk much about anything he had done in the line of duty, except briefly mentioning his rescue of John Frates.

She watched as he swam to the edge of the pool, pulled himself out and strode to a chaise to pick up his towel. Her heart slammed against her ribs because he was nude, aroused, all hard muscles and long legs, broad shoulders and male perfection.

He wrapped a towel around his middle and strode into the house. She wondered if he was angry with her for trying to probe into his past.

Their suits floated in the water and she swam to hers, pulling it on again. Then, taking his, she swam to the edge of the pool and climbed out, hurrying to get a towel and going inside to dress.

She put on a denim skirt and blouse, slipped her feet into sandals, combed her wet hair and went down to join Mike.

She found him sitting on the patio, and he came to his feet then crossed to meet her. He was in his jeans and the knit shirt again, with his wet hair combed back, giving him a sleek, dangerous look. He held out her glass of wine. "Come sit down. I'll put the steaks on in a minute. How was your day?" he asked pleasantly, as if the moments in the pool had never happened.

"An improvement. Research pays, and today was fruitful, so I hope Monday will be better than yesterday. And what about you?"

"Jessie and I had a delightful day. She's a little doll. As you know, I've never been around a baby before, much less a little girl, and she's a sweetie."

"So you two are bonding. Will wonders never cease?"

"I know, it's surprised me as much as it has you. I should have listened to you weeks ago."

"So you don't regret this marriage?"

He leaned forward, his knees touching hers, to stroke her cheek with his fingers. It was the lightest touch, yet fiery. "I haven't regretted it since the day we exchanged vows."

"I don't believe you. After the wedding, when we rode in the limo to the reception, you sounded angry and you looked anything but happy."

"Maybe then, but when we danced…" He shook his head. "From then on, no regrets."

She smiled at him, knowing he was saying only half. No regrets, but no lasting promises, either. She was still certain that in less than a year, he would walk.

"If we don't consummate the marriage, you'd have grounds for an annulment—a simple procedure," she said, looking at him over her glass as she sipped her wine.

"Consummate the marriage," he repeated, leaning close to brush kisses on her ear and neck. "We'll see about that one." He leaned away and pushed back his chair to stand. "I'll put the steaks on. I've worked up an appetite."

She stood and trailed after him into the kitchen. "What can I do?"

"Watch me cook. Talk to me."

"I mean about getting dinner ready," she said, smiling at him.

"It's ready except for the steaks. Potatoes are baked and still in the oven keeping warm. The tossed salad is in the fridge. And I have a newly baked loaf of bread."

"Helga is off today, so you did all this yourself. You're a multitalented man."

"My real talents lie elsewhere," he said.

"Oh, sugar," she teased, "I can't wait to discover your real talents!"

"I'll feed you, darlin', and then I'll show you," he said in a leering drawl that made her laugh.

They sat on the patio listening to music and talking until the steaks were done, and then they moved to the table. Slices of the fresh bread were featherlight, and the steak, when Savannah cut into it, was delicious. But her appetite fled as she gazed across the table at Mike.

The evening was a setting for seduction, and she knew it, yet in spite of that she was enjoying every moment. And the lovemaking in the pool had filled her with heated desire. She wanted to be in Mike's arms and she wanted his kisses.

They were married, and even if the marriage didn't last, he might be the love of her life. She suspected she was already in love with him, but she didn't want to study her feelings too closely yet. And if they made love, if they became husband and wife fully—in body, as well as in name—would that be a stronger tie that might bind him to her when his year was up?

If she held back, she knew that Mike wouldn't stick around all year trying to seduce her. He would move on and put her, as well as Jessie, out of his life.

She gazed across the table at him in the flickering light of the candle. His dark eyes were unfathomable, his heart locked away. She didn't know what he felt for her, if it was deep or merely physical.

He pushed back his chair and came around the table to take her hand. "Want to dance?"

Standing, she walked into his arms. "You haven't finished your dinner."

"Neither have you. I'm not hungry for steak," he said. Pulling her close, he began to dance around the patio, circling the pool while they gazed into each other's eyes. All she could see in him was unmistakable desire.

"Maybe you're changing, Mike."

"Don't count on that, Savannah. Leopards don't lose their spots. I'm not going to change."

"Maybe we're both changing."

"At least we don't clash quite as often as we did. Only half as much, I'd say," he said, and she smiled.

She ran her fingers along his jaw, feeling the smooth-shaven skin. "Thanks for taking care of Jessie so I could get my work done."

"It was an experience I wouldn't have missed for the world."

"So you'll get up with her tonight?" Savannah teased, and he looked amused.

"Today was an experience I wouldn't have missed, but I can skip the night awakenings. You wanted her badly and you knew what you were getting into, so I'll leave all that night stuff to you."

"One minute you're irresistible, Mike, and the next you're impossible."

"I take it the irresistible moments are outnumbering the impossible ones," he said, pulling her closer and dancing slowly around the patio. He periodically brushed feathery kisses across her temple.

They danced slowly while the music played over the intercom, and Savannah was barely aware of her surroundings.

In a few more minutes a fast song came on, and Mike released her, spinning her around and moving in front of her, still watching her with his smoldering gaze, making her feel utterly desirable.

She swayed, moving her hips, and wanting to tempt him to toss aside that barrier he always kept around himself.

He had gotten to her completely. He knew her background, her fears, her hopes and dreams, while his were locked away. She wanted to make him let go. She wanted him to fall in love with her. With her and with Jessie.

He danced around her, lithe, virile, too appealing. He caught her, spinning her around and then pulling her back into his arms as the piece ended. He swung her down, leaning over her to kiss her hard.

Feeling giddy and light-headed, Savannah clung to him, wanting to hold him forever. Still kissing her, he swung her up and wrapped his arms around her tightly. She pulled away to look into his eyes. They held such intensity her temperature jumped.

"You're beautiful, Savannah," he said in a husky voice, his fingers going to the top button of her blouse to twist it free. He leaned down to kiss her throat and she closed her eyes, relishing every stormy sensation he caused, running her hands over his shoulders and through his thick hair. She gasped with pleasure while he continued to twist free more buttons and trail kisses lower in the hollow between her breasts.

He shoved away her blouse and unfastened her bra to push it off, her clothing falling around her ankles while cool night air rushed over her bare skin. Mike cupped her breasts in his hands as he lowered his head to stroke her nipple with his tongue.

Clutching his shoulders, she cried out, wanting him desperately. With trembling hands, she tugged his shirt out of his jeans, pulled it over his head and tossed it aside. Eagerly, she ran her hands over his bare shoulders and chest.

"Mike," she breathed softly, knowing she was hopelessly lost.

"You're not going to turn me away tonight, Savannah," he said in her ear. "You want to make love as badly as I do. We both want to hold each other and kiss and not stop all night long."

As she wound her arms around his neck and her breasts pressed against his warm, bare chest, she knew he was right. She had fought this night, dreamed about it, worried about it, and now it was here.

"Proceed at your own risk, Mike. I want your heart. I want it all. I want you to stay and never leave."

"Shh, darlin'. The future is now. This is what we have and what we want."

"Oh, yes!" she exclaimed, standing on tiptoe to kiss him, fleetingly remembering when he had intended to fly out of Texas and her life forever, yet here he was in her arms and married to her.

His arms tightened around her, and he kissed her in return, scalding kisses that replaced thoughts and conversation with feelings and need.

She knew he intended seduction, but so did she. She wanted to make love, wanted to know him intimately, wanted to stroke and touch all of him and drive him beyond that iron-bound control he always kept.

He raised his head slightly, his dark eyes stabbing into her. "You proceed at your own risk, Savannah. I want your body."

Desire, a double-edged sword, sliced into her. Even in this there was a clash of wills, a determination in their love-making and a difference of purpose that tore at them both.

"You better guard your heart well," she said. "And remember, I've warned you." She rubbed her hips slowly against him. "You're here right now in my arms. Walk out of them now, Mike," she said while she caressed his hard manhood and then leaned down to take him into her mouth and stroke him with her tongue.

Winding his fingers tightly in her hair, he groaned. He shook and her pulse vaulted madly.

Then he reached down, his hands going beneath her arms to haul her up against him. His mouth descended possessively on hers. His tongue thrust deep, repeated thrusts that signified the sexual act, that tormented and drove her wild.

"Kiss me, Savannah," he said against her lips. "Kiss me while I love you into oblivion and demolish you with kisses," he whispered. "Do you like me to touch you here?" he asked, stroking her nipple and making her moan and cling to him.

"Do you want to be caressed and touched here?" he

whispered next. "Do you like this?" he asked as he drew circles on her stomach with his tongue,

She wound her hands in his hair and then slid her hands over him while her pounding heartbeat drowned out his voice. She had let restrictions go, and now she wanted everything with him. Exploring his hard body, she tried to give him the exquisite torment he was causing her.

Yet even in their lovemaking, she still felt that battle of wills. She wanted to seduce him into a lifetime of loving. He wanted to seduce her into his bed for the coming months.

He picked her up to carry her to a wide, padded chaise longue and lower her into it, coming down beside her to take her into his arms and kiss her while his hands roamed over her. He pushed her gently onto her stomach, moving beside her to trail kisses along her nape, his tongue stroking her, moving down her back, while his hands played over every inch of her.

He moved to the backs of her thighs, his breath warm on her sensitized skin, making her quiver. She rolled over to grasp him. "Mike, come here!" she cried as she put her arms around his neck and pulled him down for a kiss.

In moments he moved away to trail kisses down to her breasts, drawing slow circles with his tongue and then moving lower, until he was between her legs and kissing the insides of her thighs.

She opened her eyes to find Mike watching her with a look that was devastating in need. He shifted her, raising her hips, his tongue stroking her intimately where his fingers had been. She gasped and closed her eyes, her fingers clutching his shoulders.

"Mike, oh, please, come love me," she whispered.

"I want you to want me, darlin'. To really want me," he said.

She cried out, her hips arching against him while he sent her skyrocketing, one need shifting to another. Her pounding heart smothered all other sounds. She was hot, aching, wanting him.

He straightened and she looked up at him.

"Savannah, are you protected?" he asked.

"No, I'm not."

"I'll take care of it," he said, moving away to get a packet from his jeans and returning to her.

"Mike!" she gasped, coming up to take his thick shaft in her mouth and try to drive him to the same desperation she felt.

Mike tangled his fingers in her silky hair, closing his eyes, and for a minute, relishing her caresses and her tongue on him. He was burning with need for release, wanting her beyond his wildest dreams, but he was going to make this last and drive her into a frenzy of passion.

Suddenly he knew if he didn't stop her ministrations, he would lose control. He pushed her back on the chaise and stretched out beside her, caressing her, then leaning away enough to take her breast into his mouth. At last he raised his head, looking at her, certain she was the most beautiful woman on earth.

Would he ever get his fill of her? he wondered. Her skin was pearly, flawless, her cheeks pink, her lips red from his kisses. She was pink and white and blond, and her body, with its creamy, lush breasts, tiny waist and long legs, was pure temptation. He stroked her leg, his hand sliding between her thighs while he kissed her breast. She was responsive to his every touch, and a bonfire of desire for her built in him, more than for any other woman he had ever known.

Never had he wanted a woman as he did her. Never had one disturbed his sleep, caused him constant upheaval, changed his life the way she had.

He wanted to make love to her all night, wanted to make her want him the way he wanted her. He wanted all her fire and passion. Awed by her beauty, he felt as if he was under her spell. She could never imagine how many of his waking hours he thought about her, how many of his sleepless nights he ached with wanting her. She was in his erotic dreams, yet in dreams as elusive as she had been in real life—until now.

Now she was here in his arms, naked, eager, loving him in return. He slid his hands between her legs to touch, explore and stroke her while he kissed her thoroughly.

Her hands were all over him, burning him alive. Sweat poured off his body while he tried to hold back and keep control of his body.

Savannah cried out, her hips arching against Mike as she pulled him down to kiss him. He spread her legs, moving between her thighs... Suddenly he straightened.

He was on his knees between her legs, aroused, handsome, his dark hair a tangle over his forehead. His brown eyes blazed into her, and he leaned forward slightly to trail his fingertips over her breasts.

She gasped, drinking in the sight of his male perfection while he paused to get the packet, open it and slide on the condom.

And then he lowered himself to her, kissing her as she felt the warm tip of his shaft touch her lightly, tormenting her and driving her to arch her hips, while she pulled his trim buttocks in an effort to bring him closer.

"Mike," she gasped.

"I want you to really want me," he repeated, and then dipped his head to kiss her again.

She wound her arms around his neck and kissed him, and then he thrust slowly into her and withdrew and she cried out, aching for him. He thrust again, slowly filling her, hot and hard.

Her next cry was drowned by his mouth covering hers. She could feel the sweat on him, feel his pounding heart, and then all her awareness was focused on his body, his manhood.

He moved slowly, easing out and then thrusting into her, driving her wild with desire. And then his control was gone.

She moved with him, desperately trying to reach a brink, united with him at last, wanting to absorb him and wanting to give herself to him.

"Savannah, ah, darlin'!" Mike gasped. "My love!"

Above her roaring pulse, she heard him cry out her name, heard his exclamation "my love," but she knew he was in the throes of passion and not making declarations of lasting love.

And then she couldn't hear anything over her own pounding pulse. She was lost to sensation.

When release burst, she cried out his name. Colors exploded behind her tightly closed eyelids as ecstasy consumed her.

"Savannah! Darlin'," he gasped, and she felt his shuddering release.

They slowed, moving together, both drenched in sweat, hearts pounding, and gradually, her breathing began to slow. As Mike showered kisses on her face, murmuring endearments to her, she turned to him.

He kissed her—a long, slow kiss of satisfaction and union.

"You're mine at last, darlin'," he whispered, and raised his head to look at her.

She gazed into his eyes, and her heart missed a beat at the warmth she saw in the depths of brown. In that moment they were closer than ever, and she was joyous to be in his arms.

"You're beautiful," he said. "I don't want to stop holding you or kissing you or looking at you."

She stroked his jaw and smiled at him. "I don't think you can do all three at once."

"Sure I can. I'll show you," he said, kissing her and running his hand along her hip, up her rib cage.

When he raised his head, she opened her eyes. "That was two things. You couldn't look at me at the same time."

"Sure, I did. You closed your eyes. Keep them open and see." When he leaned down to kiss her again, she closed her eyes, relishing his tender, leisurely kiss. She opened her eyes when he stopped and raised his head.

"You have to keep your eyes open, Savannah," he said, smiling at her.

"I can't," she said, and they both laughed. He leaned down to nuzzle her neck.

"You're wonderful, darlin'. This was the best night of my life."

Her heart did a flip and she held him tightly, relishing both his words and the intimacy with him. "It was the best night of my life, too, Mike," she murmured solemnly, wondering how much was passion and euphoria and how much he sincerely meant. She suspected it was the former.

"Mike, this is decadent. We're on the patio...."

"It's private. We've got bushes, and beyond the bushes there's a high fence with lots of yard in between the two and lots of yard all around us before there's another house. We're as private as in my bedroom, but I vote to adjourn to the bedroom. This chaise leaves something to be desired."

"You're complaining?"

"About the chaise, not you, darlin'. Never you."

"Never until our next argument," she said with a smile, raking her fingers through his hair.

"Ah, Savannah, you're special," he said, stroking her cheek.

She smiled up at him, wondering what he really felt, knowing there was still so much of his life that was a blank to her, shut away from her and, she suspected, shut away from all others.

"You've melted my bones and I barely have strength to lift my head, but I'm going to try," he said, starting to get up, but she pulled him back into her arms. Their legs were entwined and they lay on their sides facing each other.

"Five more minutes here," she said. "Just wait. This is special, and I don't want it to end so soon."

"I had no intention of letting it end," he said softly, "but if you want to stay here a little longer, we'll stay a little longer."

He trailed his fingers down her hip to her thigh, and tingles stirred in her again. Everything he did was exciting and magical. Every touch made her want him; every smile made her melt.

He trailed kisses from her temple to her ear to her throat. She wrapped her arms around him to hold him and really kiss him, a calmer kiss, but one filled with the love she felt, yet had not told him.

She debated declaring her love, but tonight was a golden treasure, one special night, and she didn't want to do anything to tarnish it. Declaring her love for him should be good, but she feared those were not the words he wanted to hear, because he would not be able to say them back.

Placing her head on his chest, she continued to hold him tightly, thinking that for this moment he was hers—her husband, her lover. It might not last, but right now, she had it all with him.

After a few minutes, he shifted and she released him. When she did, he stood and leaned down to pick her up. Then he carried her into the house.

"I thought your bones had melted," she said.

"I'm getting a little strength back. You don't know what effort I'm expending here, but it's worth it to have such a beautiful, sexy, naked woman in my arms."

"Where are we going?" she asked, amused.

"You'll see," he replied as he headed up the stairs.

"Mike, put me down. I can walk upstairs."

"You're a feather," he said, not sounding winded at all.

"I'm impressed. Are you showing off for me? Male machismo and all that?"

"Maybe a little," he said, smiling at her. "Is it working?"

"I told you I was impressed."

He carried her to the tub in his bathroom where he turned on the hot water and in minutes had it swirling in the tub.

They bathed each other and soon Mike was aroused again. He stepped out of the tub to pull her up beside him and towel her dry, slowly drawing the soft terry cloth over her body while she did the same for him, until at last they tossed aside the towels and he pulled her into his arms to kiss her.

They made love more slowly this time. Finally, they were both lost in passion, as Mike moved her over him on his bed and stroked her breasts, while she lowered herself onto his shaft.

He was hot and hard, filling her completely, and she began to move, the sensations driving her wild. He continued to stroke her. At last she cried out her climax, collapsing on him, and then he thrust into her, shuddering with his release, his arms closing around her to hold her tightly against him.

Through the night they made love, until finally Mike slept near dawn. Savannah lay pressed to his side, his arms locked around her, and she twisted to watch him sleep. She stroked his chest and his jaw ever so lightly.

"I love you," she whispered, brushing a kiss on his throat.

His arms tightened around her and her eyes widened as she looked at him, but he still lay sleeping, his eyes closed and his breathing deep and even.

She was in love with him, wildly, totally, forever. She kissed his jaw and settled in his arms, closing her eyes to drift to sleep.

She awoke to tingling sensations and stirring desire, discovering that Mike was stroking her breasts. Looking into his brown-eyed gaze, she inhaled deeply as desire ignited in her.

When he shifted, leaning his head down to kiss her breast, circling her nipple with his tongue, she wound her fingers in his hair and moved her hips against him, feeling his hard shaft.

With all the urgency of the night before, they made love again, and after they had bathed and were back in each other's arms, Mike turned to her.

"Mike, it's six in the morning—"

"And Jessie is still sleeping, so we have a little more time to ourselves. Move in with me, Savannah."

Ten

After thinking it over, Savannah nodded. "I suppose I will, but wouldn't you rather be in the big bedroom?"

"Only if it's more fun to make love in there than in here."

"Well, the bathroom is bigger, the tub is bigger and the room has more mirrors, if that's what you want. I think you have a truly decadent streak in you."

"Nope, I just want to look at you and bathe with you and make love with you all over this enormous house. Maybe we'll try a different room every night."

She laughed. "No way. I'm not explaining changing all those beds to Helga."

"I think you have a prim streak, darlin', but thankfully, it disappears when we make love."

"You do that to me."

He smiled. "Hey, I'm starving and I remember some uneaten steaks from last night. Let's shower together and

I'll fire up the grill and heat up those steaks. We can eat them now. I might scramble some eggs to go with them.''

"Now there's a healthy breakfast," she said.

"It's damned healthy. Makes you strong and able to roll around in the sack for hours at a time."

She laughed and he hugged her close. "Savannah, this is good. Not lions and tigers at all."

"I don't know. I'd say I had a tiger in bed last night."

He chuckled and stood, reaching to pick her up, but she slipped away from him, swiftly wrapping the sheet around her and heading out of the room.

"You shower in here and I'll shower in my room, because I'm famished and if we shower together, we won't get to eat. Jessie might wake up anytime now."

"Spoilsport," he called as she hurried out of the room.

When Jessie awoke, Mike got her and insisted on feeding her. Savannah watched him with the baby, marveling at the change in him, loving him with all her heart and wondering how much more he could change. Could he fall in love?

They spent the day playing with Jessie, but the sexual tension between them began to build, and by dinner, Savannah was looking forward to being alone with him again.

When Jessie was down for the night, they moved into the master bedroom and made love until the early hours of the morning.

On Monday, Mike took Jessie to his mother-in-law's house, and he and Savannah both returned to work.

Wednesday night, when Savannah got home from work, she bathed and changed into cutoffs and a T-shirt. About an hour later, Mike returned home, entering the downstairs family room where she was playing with Jessie. He was in a navy suit and Savannah's pulse jumped at the sight of him. She got up to greet him, winding her arms around his neck and standing on tiptoe to kiss him soundly.

His arm banded her waist and they kissed until they heard Jessie banging a toy on the floor. They stopped to look at the baby, and then they smiled at each other. "How're my girls?" Mike asked in a husky voice. Keeping his arm around Savannah's waist, he crossed the room with her to pick up Jessie, who held out her arms, clearly begging to be hugged, too.

"We're both fine," Savannah replied. "Constance called and said her dad is much better. She thinks she can come back to work next week, although Mom is beginning to like keeping Jessie."

Mike smiled at Savannah. "Well, we have something to celebrate tonight. I solved my first case today. Wyatt will get his horses back. They won't even have to hold the horses for evidence, because Gandy had a lot of stolen goods, and the sheriff is letting Wyatt take his animals home."

"Congratulations!" she said, smiling at him. Then she caught Mike's wrist. "We can *really* celebrate tonight. I haven't told you the best yet. Mike, the court date is set for the adoption!" she exclaimed. "I guess with us married and you already her guardian and all the connections I have in the legal system, this moved through quickly."

Her eyes sparkled, and he caught her up to swing her around in his arms, laughing with her. "You got your way, Savannah. Jessie will be your baby. When's the date?"

"A week from Friday," she said, thinking that would be one of the happiest days of her life. The wedding, loving Mike, adopting Jessie—all were wonderful, joyous happenings, and she felt incredibly blessed. And if Mike walked after Jessie was adopted? She looked at him, hoping he would stay, because both she and Jessie seemed to be more important to him with each passing day.

She warned herself that she might be looking at the world through rose-colored glasses, wrapped in euphoria from his lovemaking and the adoption.

The Friday of the following week, as they stood before Judge Delancy Taggert, Savannah had butterflies in her stomach. Never in any trial had she been this nervous. She was afraid something would happen to keep the adoption from going through. Even though she knew everything was set and all the red tape had been cleared up to this point.

Both Mike's and her parents were present. All the rest of her family was also present, but Mike's brothers hadn't been able to make it this soon after the wedding.

Jessie was dressed in a pale-blue dress with a matching bow in her hair, and Savannah thought she looked beautiful. Savannah was holding her, but when she began to fuss, Mike took her, and she curled up in his arms and went to sleep. Savannah glanced at him. He looked handsome, dangerous, sexy. Yet when he looked at Jessie, his tender expression melted Savannah's heart.

And then they had to rise for the judge, and the proceedings commenced. It was far simpler than Savannah expected and soon over. They signed papers, witnesses signed papers, and then the judge declared that they were legal parents of Jessie Frates, whose name was changed to Jessie Remington.

It was over and Jessie was her baby. Hers and Mike's. Savannah took the baby from Mike and held her close while court was adjourned. Then all the family crowded around to give congratulations. Savannah looked at Mike, standing nearby. He seemed relaxed, happy, and she wondered what he was thinking. This was supposed to have been the moment that would give him his freedom. His gaze met hers, and he smiled and gave her a thumbs-up.

They went back to the Frates mansion for a catered celebration, and it wasn't until nine o'clock that night that the last guest left.

Mike picked up Jessie to carry her to bed and Savannah went with him. "I'm sorry your parents couldn't stay longer," she said. "It was a long trip for them to be here such a short time."

"They already had a cruise planned, so they have to get

back for it or cancel it. They promised to come back here in a month.'' Mike looked down at Jessie in his arms. ''This was a big day in her young life. She doesn't know it, but it was,'' Mike said. ''And a big day for us. And when I put her in her bed, you and I can begin to celebrate.''

The phone rang and Savannah answered it, talked a minute and then handed the phone to Mike.

''It's Wyatt. He wants to talk to you. Probably wants to thank you again.''

She kissed Jessie and tiptoed out, finding Mike still on the phone, which he had carried to the upstairs family room. When he told Wyatt goodbye, he turned to her. ''Did you know about that?''

''About what?''

''Wyatt wants to show his gratitude. Besides paying my fee, he wants to give me that damned stallion.''

She laughed. ''You can keep it at my folks' and ride it when we go out there on Saturdays.''

''Listen, you,'' Mike said in a mock-threatening voice, crossing the room to sit beside her on the sofa and look her in the eye. ''Who's been telling people about my ability to ride?''

''Well, after all, you did stay on Jester, and few can say that.''

''Yeah, well, Wyatt heard about it and knows how much your family enjoys riding, so he wants to give me the stallion as a token of appreciation. He's already talked to your dad about keeping the horse at their place.''

''So why are you unhappy? Scared of the legend that whoever has the white stallion finds true love?''

''Hell, no. I didn't even think about the legend. I just don't want Wyatt to give me a horse. I charged him plenty for finding the animal. It's like this inheritance from John Frates. I was just doing my job.''

''People are grateful,'' she said. ''I think you're scared

because if you take the horse...well, you know the legend.
You might be in love forever.''

Mike looked at her twinkling eyes. ''Savannah, you're
laughing at me. So help me...'' He pushed her down on the
sofa to tickle her, and she screeched and laughed and
kicked, protesting loudly.

In minutes he sat up and pulled her onto his lap. ''I'm
not scared of a horse, and I can't get out of taking the horse
any more than I could get out of taking this inheritance.
Here I am with a wife and a baby because a man was grateful to me for doing what I got paid to do. Now I'm going
to have a horse because of that.''

She giggled again, and he nuzzled her neck and rubbed
his stubbly jaw across her cheek. She laughed and tried to
wriggle away, and then they looked into each other's eyes
and the moment transformed. He bent his head to kiss her
until they were both breathless. Mike carried Savannah to
their bedroom to make love to her.

Later, Savannah lay in his arms while he slept. She
thought about Wyatt giving the stallion to Mike. She didn't
believe in the old legend, either, but she wished it was true
and wished that when Mike became the owner of the horse,
true love would come into his life.

On Saturday, Savannah's family all stood watching while
Mike saddled the white stallion and rode around the corral
for the first time. Everyone applauded, and then Savannah
and her family mounted their own horses and headed out.
Mike moved along with them.

''Wyatt said this horse can be ridden, but I think for our
usual Saturday morning rides, I better go back to Bluebonnet,'' he told Savannah. ''I feel like I'm holding a lot of
energy in check. I suspect this horse would like nothing
better than a good run.''

''You can do that. We'll catch the others later.'' She
called to Lucius and motioned them to go on.

"Since Jester, your two younger brothers have more or less accepted me, but I don't think Lucius ever will."

"Oh, yes, he will, and if he doesn't, don't worry about it. I told you, you can take care of yourself where Lucius is concerned, I'm sure."

"Yeah, right," Mike said. "He's bigger than I am, taller, and he's got anger on his side."

"Don't be scared of my big brother," she teased in a patronizing voice. His dark eyes flashed.

"You're asking for it, Savannah. I know why you're a lawyer. You like the fight."

"No, I don't. I certainly don't want to fight with you. Now here," she said, leading him to a pasture that was flat ground. "I'll race you to that oak, and you'll see what your stallion can do."

"All right. You say go. You get a head start, because I think this horse can outrun yours easily."

"We'll see," she said smugly, and Mike grinned.

"You always have to challenge me, Savannah."

"You bring that out in me," she answered smoothly. "Winner gets to decide how we spend the evening and where."

His brows arched. "Now that's a prize! If I win, I want your folks to keep Jessie tonight so I can have you all to myself."

"Oh, my! You might cause me to want to throw the race. All right, Mike, get ready, set—" she turned her horse "—go!" With that she urged her horse into a gallop.

Mike gave the stallion his head, and the big horse pulled ahead of Savannah's mount to win by a length. They reined in and she was laughing. Mike's heart thudded and he wanted to pull her down on the ground and take her now, but he knew they might not have privacy. But it wouldn't matter for a kiss. He rode close to her. "I get what I want tonight, Savannah," he said. "Can you ask your folks to keep Jessie?"

"You know they'd love to," she said. She gestured at the stallion. "That's your horse, Mike. He likes you."

"I'll tell you what *I* like," Mike said, moving the stallion close to her and standing in the stirrups to lean over and kiss her.

Savannah wound her arms around his neck to return his kiss, thinking she would never get enough of him. Every day with him she loved him more. She wished she could weave a spell of love around him where he would never want to leave her.

Finally, Mike's horse shifted and Mike released her. As he leaned down to catch her reins for her, he looked into her face, and she saw there the promises of the night to come.

She straightened her shirt and took the clip out of her hair, shaking her head and letting her hair fall over her shoulders. "Want to race back? Another hard run ought to wear him down a little."

"Sure, let's go," Mike said, turning his horse and urging him forward. He galloped across the pasture with Savannah beside him, then let the stallion pull ahead. The stallion was a powerful animal, and Mike still wished Wyatt hadn't been so generous. He reined the horse in and waited for Savannah.

"He may be wild," Mike said, "but he's got stamina."

"You or the horse?"

"The horse," Mike answered dryly. "There's nothing wild about me."

"Not much, there isn't! And I saw that Harley you have in the garage now."

"I'll give you a ride whenever you want."

"No, thank you. Come with me and let me show you a part of this place I like, and the horses can have a drink."

They rode past a grove of scrub oaks and then entered another stand of oaks, where they rode in tandem until they reached a clearing on a creek bank. Savannah dismounted and led her horse to the creek to let him drink, and Mike did the same.

Savannah breathed the cool morning air. Her nerves hummed with excitement, and she was aware of Mike only a few feet away. She looked at the clear, swift-running creek that she had loved since she was a child.

"The horses will be all right here. Let's go to the top of the hill—there's a great view." She crossed the stream, stepping from rock to rock. In the middle she stopped to glance back at Mike, who looked pale and stricken.

"Mike? Are you all right?" she asked.

He blinked and shook his head. "I'm fine. Savannah, let's go back and join the others." He mounted and turned his horse to ride away.

She didn't know what had happened, but she knew something was wrong. In silence she mounted her horse and moved up beside him, noticing that a muscle tightened in his jaw and his fists were clenched.

They turned the horses to follow the creek, and by the time they reached her family, Mike was his usual self, acting as if nothing unusual had happened.

When they rejoined the others, Mike was aware that Lucius gave him a long, intent look, then turned his gaze to Savannah. At last Lucius resumed his ride, but the rest of the morning and over lunch, Mike thought Lucius had lost some of his animosity.

When he was in the car with Savannah going home, he told her and she laughed as he drove.

"You have a smudge of my makeup on your shirt collar, and I came back with my hair down and my shirt wrinkled, so he probably guessed we were off by ourselves and kissing. Also, we asked my folks to keep Jessie tonight so you and I can have the evening to ourselves. That sounds like people who have more than a paper-only marriage."

"So it does," Mike said, becoming solemn again in a day that had been relaxed and fun and filled with anticipation for the night ahead. "Why didn't you tell me I had makeup on my collar?"

"It's nothing much, and I don't think you can get it off without washing the shirt, so I didn't see any point in telling you. Besides, aren't you glad that Lucius likes you now?"

"That just makes my day," he said, and she wondered about him. He was cooler than he had been, both to her and her family.

Then while they talked and he seemed to relax again, she forgot about his puzzling behavior and her attention shifted to the night ahead.

At home in the early evening, they swam for an hour and then Mike grilled steaks, which they ate on the patio.

Savannah was acutely aware of Mike in his brief navy swim trunks, able to remember in total detail how he looked naked.

And drawing her to him just as much as his high-caliber sexuality was his increasing attention to Jessie. All through lunch today at her parents' house, Mike had held Jessie on his lap. When they had ambrosia salad, Mike had cut bites of oranges into tiny pieces and fed them to Jessie—she'd never had table food before and smacked her lips eagerly.

"This is a life I never dreamed of," he said quietly now. "Come here, Savannah."

She moved to his lap and he wrapped his arms around her. She leaned down to kiss him, and within moments, his hands were sliding the straps of her swimsuit down her arms. She leaned away.

"I don't care how much privacy we have here. It's broad daylight and you're not undressing me out here for the world to see."

He looked amused as he stood and lifted her in his arms, carrying her into the house. As soon as they stepped through the door, he set her on her feet and pulled her into his embrace to kiss her. This time when he slid her suit down her arms, she didn't stop him.

Their suits had dried since they'd climbed out of the pool, and now her suit dropped around her ankles. She kicked it away while she peeled away his suit and freed him of its constraints.

Mike leaned down, taking her nipple into his mouth, to stroke and draw lazy circles around the tip with his tongue. She gasped, fiery tingles centering low in her body. She wanted him with increasing urgency.

She wound her fingers in his hair and then slid her hands over his muscled chest down his abdomen to his manhood, and began stroking the thick shaft.

Winding his fingers in her hair, Mike groaned and whispered her name until he stopped her, catching her hands to hold them up and kiss her wrists and then her fingers.

"I want you now, Savannah," he said gruffly, pausing to grab a condom and then picking her up and carrying her to the thick rug in the family room, where he lowered her to the floor. He stretched out on his back, pulling her over him and settling her on his shaft.

Tremors shook her and she abandoned herself to passion, moving with him, while he caressed her breasts and drove her to a frenzy.

"Mike!" she cried out, moving wildly, feeling him arch tightly beneath her, and then he pulled away, moving her.

"Mike!" she gasped. "Please!"

He moved between her legs and entered her, kissing her and then pausing. "I want your legs tighter around me, darlin'. I want all your warmth around me."

His head came down as he kissed her again and she arched her hips, tightening her legs around him, clinging to his back. They moved together as he carried her over the brink and she crashed into sheer rapture.

"Mike!" she cried again, clutching him and spinning away in ecstasy. "I love you," she said softly.

She felt his release and then he held her tightly in his

arms, still moving with her, slowing while they both tried to catch their breaths.

When they quieted, he rolled onto his side, holding her close and keeping her with him. "Ahh, darlin'. I've been dreaming about that all day long. We have a long, grand night ahead of us."

She traced his jaw with her finger, realizing he had shaved again when he'd changed into his swim trunks. She settled in his arms, content to take the present and not think about tomorrow.

"You have a nice family, Savannah. I wish you could get to know mine. They're nice folks, too."

"I'm sure they are," she said. "They'd have to be to have raised such a super son." He nuzzled her neck, tickling her and making her giggle. "I meant that, but I'm going to take it back if you keep tickling me!"

He leaned away to smile at her, stroking long, silken strands of her hair away from her face. "This is really good, Savannah. I'm glad you twisted my arm into this."

She made a face at him. "I didn't have to twist your arm to get you naked on the floor here with me."

"No, you didn't. Darlin', this is good and I'm glad I hung around Texas."

She wanted to ask him if it was so good that he would continue to hang around Texas, but she didn't. Instead, she again stroked his jaw with her fingers. "Mike, you keep a lot of yourself shut away from me."

He shifted to look at her. "Only the bad parts. The parts you don't want to know."

"Maybe they wouldn't be so bad," she said quietly, "if you shared them with somebody."

That shuttered look came over his features and an expression of pain, and Savannah remembered this morning at the stream.

"I don't want to pry, but I want you to trust me." She was lying on her back with her side pressed against him.

"I trust you," he said gruffly. "
ber." He gazed beyond her. "There'
lo. There's no way anyone can help."

"Yes, there is. It always helps to talk i

He played with her hair and was silen
hought maybe he'd dozed off. Then, "Colin a   n
neighboring West Texas ranches. There was a cre   n our
ranch, and Colin and I used to cross the creek the way you
did this morning."

As he talked, Mike's words slowed and his voice became
more raspy. "Sometimes memories come back as clear as
if it were yesterday, and then it hurts all over again. Maybe
not as badly as when he was killed, but it hurts," Mike said,
grinding out the words while a muscle worked in his jaw.

He fell silent again and she didn't push. If he wanted to
tell her, he would, and if he didn't, he wouldn't.

He rolled onto his back and flung his arm up to shield
his eyes. "He shouldn't have died. That's what makes it so
terrible. I should have saved him."

"What happened?"

Mike was quiet and she waited, turning on her side to
hold him close.

"We had a covert assignment—all four of us, Jonah,
Boone, Colin and me—to get an agent, a spy who had been
taken hostage. There is still a double agent—as far as I
know, he was never caught—but he blew our cover, as well
as that of the man we were to rescue, which is why he was
a hostage." Mike paused and she continued to wait in silence, hurting for him.

"Colin went in first. The three of us were behind when
he slipped into the house. Our cover had been blown, but
we didn't know it. Someone set off a bomb and it killed
Colin and the hostage and the men holding him. The ter-
rorist leader was the only one who escaped. It was a car
bomb that exploded. The car was parked only feet away

where they were," Mike said in a rasp. He paused and Savannah held him tightly.

"Everything was smoke and flames, sirens blazing. We were on a covert mission so we had to get out of there."

"You can't help what happened," Savannah said.

"Damn straight I could have. I should have noticed the car. A man drove up, parked, got out and walked away, and I was so intent on watching Colin and following him into the house, I didn't think. That kind of deadly mistake shouldn't happen. I should have noticed the car. I didn't even go look for Colin's body because we had to get out of there."

"Mike, you can't blame yourself and you know he wouldn't want you to feel this way."

"I tell myself that, but it doesn't change a thing."

He wrapped his arms around her. "Colin was like one of my brothers. His parents have aged over his loss, and they'll always hurt."

"From what you've told me, you shouldn't blame yourself."

"I tell myself I shouldn't, but in my heart I do and I always will. It's a damned nightmare I have sometimes. And Colin and I were so close. Seeing you jump from rock to rock in that stream today—I saw Colin do that a hundred times. Out of the blue, something will remind me of him and then pain slices into me like a knife. It hurts to lose someone you love."

She kissed his shoulder. "It does hurt terribly to lose someone you love," she confirmed quietly.

"I guess you understand about loss and hurt as well as any soldier," he said.

"Mike, you might not have saved Colin, but you saved Jessie."

"She would have had a good enough life. Nothing like this, but okay."

"Instead, you've given her a huge gift. Don't be so hard

on yourself about Colin.'' Savannah ran her hands over him, kissing him lightly until he turned to look at her and he smiled.

"Thanks, Savannah, for listening. Want to shower and swim?''

"Sure," she answered, feeling closer to him than she ever had and knowing he had just revealed a lot of himself to her that he'd probably never shared with anyone else before. Also, she realized that Mike might be as scared to love as she had been.

He stood and picked her up easily, carrying her to a downstairs bathroom and setting her on her feet in the shower with him. As warm water splashed over them and he began to soap her, she knew it would be some time before they swam....

That night Mike held Savannah in his arms while he lay awake. He shifted slightly to look at her, curled in his arms, locks of her hair spilling over the pillow. Carefully, he stroked a strand away from her cheek. She was so incredibly soft. Soft, warm, all curves. Full of fire and mischief and determination. He had heard her twice say, "I love you," to him. Neither time had she thought he would hear her.

She wasn't the first woman to tell him that, but it was the first time that the words had meant something to him. What did he feel for Savannah? He had a job in Washington waiting for him, his old life to go back to.

He thought about holding Jessie in his arms and her laughter and her smiles when he entered the room.

And Savannah—no woman had ever excited him the way she did. No woman had ever been as beautiful. Silken nights, constant excitement, someone who cared. What was he going back to? His solitary life, total freedom to do what he wanted. Did his freedom outweigh the other? Could he walk away from Savannah and Jessie now even if he wanted to?

He ran his fingers lightly down her arm and leaned down to brush a kiss on her temple. "I love you," he mouthed silently, wondering if he really was in love with her. Love could hurt. But love was the good part of life.

Mike lay back, putting his arm beneath his head and staring into the dark, thinking about Savannah and Jessie, searching his heart for what he truly felt. Soon he would have to make choices, and when the time came to do so, he better know what he wanted.

Two days later, as Mike left the offices of V. R. Hunsacker, he made notations in a ledger he carried. Closing the ledger, Mike wondered how Savannah would react to his suspicions.

Over dinner that evening, he gazed at her, half-inclined to wait another day before telling her what he suspected. They were in euphoria, wanting each other constantly, making love as often as possible. He didn't want shoptalk to destroy their happiness. He didn't want to make Savannah unhappy, and he suspected his discoveries were going to make her very unhappy. She looked beautiful tonight, dressed in cutoffs and a blue knit shirt, her hair down.

As they ate, he decided to go ahead and tell her. "I've learned a few things about the clients you've recently lost."

"You sound serious. What have you learned?"

"All the clients you've lost have gone with the same firm."

Savannah arched her brows. "That's odd. What firm is it?"

"A new firm out of Austin. It's Plunkett, Paine, and Marshall Associates."

"I don't know any of those names."

"You wouldn't. They're not from these parts. Jeb Plunkett is from Dallas, Morgan Paine is from Houston, and Ty Marshall is from Kansas City."

Savannah shook her head. "I don't know. I've never had

any dealings with them. How could they lure away our clients when they're so new?''

"I looked into their backgrounds, and these men have not been tremendously successful in the past. One is basically an ambulance chaser. One has been investigated about ethics, but nothing came of it.''

"Why would our clients go with a firm like that?''

"That's what I'm wondering. It can't be coincidence. Someone recommended this firm highly to get those companies to switch their business. It wasn't those guys. They're not local and they don't have the contacts.''

She rubbed her forehead. "I can't imagine.''

"Do you have any enemies, Savannah?'' Mike asked quietly.

"No! Well, I take that back. Any person who's been defeated is unhappy with the lawyer who won, whether it's a settlement or a trial. Yes, I guess there're plenty of people who aren't happy with me or with Troy and who have the assets to try to cause us trouble.''

"Can you make me a list of ones from this year?''

"I suppose, but it'll be incomplete, and frankly, it seems ridiculous. People don't go to that much trouble to get even with their opponent's lawyers. They don't like us, but we're not usually the main target.''

"True,'' Mike said. "So that leaves another possibility.''

"You think it's someone from our own firm?'' She shook her head. "No way. Liz and Nathan seem happy, and I can't imagine they would have enough clout to change the legal staff of three corporations. Troy wouldn't, because it would be like stealing from himself. He wouldn't do that to me any more than I would do that to him. I work with him daily.''

"Did he still want to date you up until the time you married me?''

"Yes, but that's not a big deal. We haven't been on a date in two years. And then it was never anything serious.''

"I'm glad to hear that," Mike said.

She arched her eyebrows again. "Why would you care?"

He shrugged. "I care. I'm not the jealous type, but I don't like Troy Slocum and I'm glad you didn't date him much."

Savannah smiled, pleased, and wondering what Mike's feelings for her were. She was surprised that it bothered him to know that she and Troy had dated. "It's not my partner or associates. It has to be someone else."

Mike dropped the subject, more interested in pulling Savannah into his arms. Jessie had gone down early tonight and he had Savannah to himself right now. He didn't want to spend the time discussing business. He reached for her.

"You're not eating, anyway. Come sit in my lap," he said.

Her blue eyes changed, a sensual look coming into them. She pushed back her chair, got up and came around to him, then sat on his lap and wrapped her arms around his neck.

On Tuesday, Mike called Savannah from his office. "I'm going to be gone tonight and tomorrow on a job. I'll call and give you my hotel tonight, but my cell phone is always on."

"I'll miss you, Mike," she said, knowing she would miss him terribly.

"I'll miss you, darlin', and if I can get home sooner, I will. Give Jessie a kiss for me. I wish I could give *you* a kiss right now."

"Hurry home."

Mike said goodbye, thankful she hadn't asked what job he was working on. He had an unpleasant task ahead of him, and he suspected it was going to have unhappy results. He had a bad feeling about Savannah's firm losing business. He suspected Savannah would know the person causing it quite well.

On Wednesday after work, Savannah hurried home to relieve Constance of Jessie's care, feeding the baby and playing with her. Savannah changed to cutoffs and a T-shirt, fastening her hair behind her head with a ribbon. She missed Mike terribly and she loved him more every day. She prayed he would fall in love with her and with Jessie. She knew that daily she and Jessie were becoming more important to him, yet he was a tough, solitary man who had never had or wanted a long-lasting relationship, much less marriage.

When she heard a car, she scooped up Jessie to carry her to the back door. Her heart leaped at the sight of Mike climbing out of the car and approaching the house in long strides. If she hadn't been holding Jessie, she would have run and thrown herself into his arms.

He hugged her and Jessie, then kissed them both. The baby held her arms out and Mike took her, holding her close with one arm while he draped his other arm around Savannah's shoulders. They went back into the house.

"Let me take care of Jessie tonight, okay?" he said.

"That means feeding her."

"Fine with me. And then when she's asleep, I have plans for you and me."

Savannah smiled.

Mike fed and changed Jessie, lying on the floor in the family room to play with her until she took her last bottle and he rocked her to sleep. He returned to the family room and switched off all the lights but a small one in the bar. Then he crossed the room to pull Savannah into his arms.

The following morning, before Constance had arrived and while Jessie was still asleep, Mike turned to look at Savannah, who was pulling on her skirt and had already fastened the buttons on her green blouse.

"Have lunch with me today," he said. "We need to talk."

"This sounds serious," she said. "Business?"

He nodded and she realized he was worried. "What is it?" she asked.

"We both have to go to work, and Jessie could wake any

minute. I think I should tell you at lunch. Actually, I meant to tell you last night.''

''Now you have to tell me,'' she said curiously as she crossed the room and put her arms around his waist. ''What is it?''

''You're not going to like it.''

''Try me,'' she said, barely thinking about business. Most of her attention was on him and how in love she was with him. She wished they could just stay home all day and not have to see anyone else except Jessie. ''Mike, I'm so glad you like Jessie.''

''Of course, I like her. Savannah, pay attention. I know who has the tie to that new law company.''

Eleven

"**I** saw those three men in the firm in Austin and they were having lunch with Troy."

Savannah stared at Mike, then shook her head in disbelief. "No. You're wrong. Troy wouldn't do that to me. He might have found them just like you did and wants to get to know them for business reasons, but not what you're talking about."

"I think Troy is the one who is behind your loss of clients," Mike said, pulling on his charcoal suit coat.

"I'm sure he can explain having lunch with them."

"I'd rather you didn't confront him with it yet. I want to check into some more things. Do you have an agreement where, if either of you leaves the firm, you can't take clients with you?"

"Yes, we do, but you're wrong, Mike. Troy and I have known each other for years. It was out of mutual respect and trust that we went into business together."

"You've told me that your firm was almost nothing when

you both started and John Frates's business really gave you a boost.''

''That's true, but Troy wouldn't lure away our people to help another agency. I know he wouldn't,'' she said, moving away from Mike and thinking about what he had told her. ''I'm as sure of that as I'm sure of myself. And it doesn't make sense, either. It hurts him financially as much as it hurts me.''

''You might be wrong. Let me check a little further before you talk to him,'' Mike repeated.

''He'll have a good reason for being with those Austin attorneys. I trust Troy like a brother. You back off and leave him alone.''

''You're being stubborn again,'' Mike said.

''You can't imagine how absurd *you're* being. The man is not going to rip off the company he's in.''

''He might if he can make a lot more money elsewhere. Or if he's angry because you wouldn't date him. Savannah, you listen to your heart more than your head,'' Mike said, becoming annoyed with her and remembering how stubborn she'd been when they'd first met. ''It makes sense. You've lost clients. They've all gone with one company that's new. You don't know any of the lawyers in the firm and Troy has had lunch with them. Will you stop and think logically?''

''You're the one who isn't thinking logically. Troy wouldn't do that to me, and if he did, he would be hurting himself as much as me. You just don't like him. Forget Troy or get off the case.''

''Even if Troy is the one sabotaging your firm?''

''I simply know he's not. I'm going to ask him.''

''You're so damned stubborn, Savannah.''

''No one can be more stubborn than you are,'' she retorted.

They glared at each other. Suddenly Jessie's crying came over the intercom, and Savannah went to tend to her. When

Constance arrived, Savannah returned to the master bedroom and found it empty.

She wanted to tell Mike to forget the case, yet she knew she needed to find out if someone was deliberately trying to sabotage the firm. But she was sure it wasn't Troy, and she intended to ask him about his acquaintance with the attorneys in Austin.

That evening, she waited for Mike to get home, glad when Jessie took a late nap so she could talk to Mike without interruption.

Savannah was on the patio when he came striding out. He had changed into jeans and a T-shirt, and in spite of her anger with him, her pulse still jumped at the sight of him.

He sat down facing her, studying her intently. "So he gave you a good excuse," Mike said.

"What makes you think that?"

"It shows. You look happy, smug even. If he hadn't been able to talk his way out of it, you'd be upset."

"Yes, I would have, but Troy had a perfectly logical answer. He's been investigating on his own—he's used a private detective—and he wanted to meet those attorneys and talk to them. You just happened to see him on the day he met with them."

"And you believed him," Mike said.

"Yes, I did. I want you to leave Troy alone. Stop following him."

"There's no need to now. You've alerted him to what I'm doing."

"And when you do, it won't be Troy and you'll owe both me and Troy an apology."

"Maybe you, never Troy. And I don't see any need in arguing over apologies because I don't think I'm going to have to make any."

"You can be insufferably sure of yourself."

"I'm not the only one, Savannah," he said, standing and

staring at her. A muscle worked in his jaw, and in that moment she realized that she was going to lose him.

When he turned and left, she was tempted to call after him, but she bit her lip, kept quiet and let him go.

She could go after him, tell him to go ahead and investigate Troy. Would that smooth things over and put them back where they had been? She doubted it. Mike was inordinately stubborn, yet if he persisted, he would find if someone was deliberately causing her to lose clients and he would find that it wasn't Troy.

By the time he discovered the truth, irreparable harm might have already been done to their relationship because already the golden glow they had been wrapped in was gone. Savannah hurt and wondered if it was worth it to defend Troy to the extent that she lost Mike, yet she knew she had never really had Mike anyway.

Hours past midnight she lay in the big bed all alone and wondered where he was sleeping—or if he was sleeping. Was he as miserable as she was?

By Friday, Mike hardly saw Savannah alone. He saw her when they were both with Jessie, but those were the only times. He knew he had to make some decisions, because his investigation of Troy had angered her beyond anything he could have imagined. He would have thought she was in love with the guy, except she had been firm about refusing to date Troy, and there was no reason for her to tell him anything except the truth.

Did he want to go back to his life in Washington? Mike mulled it over, wondering if he wound up proving to Savannah that it was Troy sabotaging the firm, she would hate him for it.

Mike knew that if he left Savannah, he would be tied forever to Jessie. He couldn't walk away from the little girl now. She was his. She bore his name and she was his daughter legally, and as far as Mike was concerned, she really was his daughter.

He loved her. He didn't have to question his feelings for Jessie at all. It was impossible not to love her.

He always came back around to what he felt for Savannah. How deep did his feelings run and could they survive this latest, big clash?

When the weekend came, he packed and flew to Washington, renewing acquaintances, returning to his old life. Saturday night, as he switched off the lights in his hotel room and looked out the window at the city he loved, he ached with longing for Savannah.

Savannah didn't hear from Mike all weekend or for all of Monday. She didn't know where he was and wondered if he had gone back to Washington to rethink his life.

She missed him more than she'd thought possible and now she wished she hadn't fought with him about Troy. She no longer cared, although she knew she should. The firm wasn't as important as home and family. Family had always been the most important thing in her life and it still was. She missed Mike, knew Jessie missed him, and it wasn't worth defending Troy to lose Mike. Time would tell whether Troy was involved with the law firm in Austin.

Mike's absence might not be about the issue of Troy at all. Jessie was adopted now, and according to their agreement, that was all Mike had to stick around for; he was free. The fact that they had become physically intimate, Savannah suspected, wouldn't, in Mike's view, change anything in their agreement.

She wondered whether he would come back to Texas or if he'd already walked out of her life, not to return for a long time and then only to get the divorce.

By midmorning, Savannah knew her mind wasn't on work. In an uncustomary move, she gave up trying to work and told the receptionist she was going home. She sent Constance home, because the only thing Savannah wanted was to be with Jessie.

In early afternoon, when Jessie had gone down for her nap, Savannah wandered around the huge house, remembering Mike in every room she entered. She was tempted to try to find him, just to talk to him, but she knew that was futile. If he had made up his mind to leave, she wouldn't be able to talk him out of it. Nor would she even want to.

He either loved her and would return or he wouldn't. She thought he loved Jessie, but even if he did love Jessie, that would not be enough to get him to return to Texas if he wanted out of the marriage.

Savannah was certain Mike wasn't in Texas. She'd called his office early this morning and gotten no answer. She had his cell-phone number and could call him on that, but she was reluctant. If he had left Texas for Washington, then he was thinking about leaving her, and she knew she had to let him go.

That was their agreement, and she had walked into their relationship with her eyes wide open and fully knowing that he wasn't into lasting commitment. He had warned her from the first that he wasn't, yet why did she think what they had was unique, once-in-a-lifetime special? Probably every woman who had loved him had thought the same thing.

She had thought about calling him to tell him that she no longer cared whether he investigated Troy or not. Yet she knew that doing so wouldn't change anything, because there would always be issues between them where they didn't agree and each one thought the other incredibly stubborn and willful. It always came back to the fact that they were too much alike in some ways.

Savannah wiped away tears, realizing it was the first time in her life she had cried over a man. She was hurting and she wanted Mike back, and she wished she could undo what she had done, yet she knew Troy wasn't the real issue. Sooner or later, Mike had to make a decision just as she had made a decision about this marriage, a marriage that had started without love and was only a means to an end. For her it had turned into love, and she had wanted Mike to feel the same.

"Mike," she whispered, looking out the window and wishing she would see him coming up the drive, but the drive was as empty as her heart.

As he flew back to Texas, Mike stared out the window of the plane. He could only see images of Savannah, not the blue sky or clouds. Never had he felt this way about a woman. A million times each day he thought about her. Too many times to count over the weekend, he had reached for the phone to call her, only to stop at the last moment. He missed her and wanted her, and he wanted to go back to Texas to the life they'd had before he'd laid out his suspicions about Troy.

Yet Mike was certain he was right about Troy. He just had to figure a way to prove it.

If Troy was tearing up their firm, what did he have to gain that was so much better than remaining partners with Savannah? Mike knew he needed to be able to answer that question.

He wondered about the firm's finances and if he could get Savannah to hire an outside accountant to audit her books.

If Troy was the guilty party, would that kill any chance Mike had of getting back with Savannah?

Should he give up his investigation into the loss of clients? Mike knew he either had to prove it was Troy or resign from the job before he could expect to get back together with Savannah.

It was impossible to think long about Troy, because Savannah dominated his thoughts and dreams. Mike ached for her, thought about her constantly.

All weekend he had hardly slept. Each night when he

finally went to bed, he would lie in the dark and hurt, wanting Savannah in his arms.

He could drop his pursuit of Troy. Was that as important as his relationship with Savannah? Savannah was financially secure, so why was this such an issue?

Mike knew that it angered him that she didn't trust him. She had taken Troy's side against him and, to Mike's thinking, unreasonably so. And they would always clash because they were both willful. So it got back to making up his mind which life he wanted—his old one in Washington or his new one in Texas with Savannah and Jessie. A solitary life versus a life of love. It wasn't a difficult choice.

Mike wondered what Savannah was doing right now. He looked at the sky and thought about Savannah under the same sky, so far away in Texas.

In passion she had whispered, "I love you." Words he had never told her or any other woman. Yet he knew now that he did love Savannah, that he wanted her back in his arms and in a real marriage.

He raked his fingers through his hair and reached for the airline phone on the back of the seat in front of him. Then he realized he wanted to talk to her in person, not on an airplane phone from a thousand miles away.

He loved his wife and he missed her, and today he was going back to Texas and hopefully tonight he could tell her. But there was something he needed to do first.

When Savannah didn't hear from Mike on Monday, and then Tuesday came, she was certain he'd decided to return to Washington and his former life. Unable to concentrate and hurting badly, she took another day off work. Several times during the day, she reached for the phone to call Mike, but each time she stopped, knowing he'd made his decision and talking to him wouldn't change it.

Late in the afternoon, Savannah heard a car and raced to

the window to look out. Her heart thudded when she saw Mike's car go around the house to park in back.

She raced through the house, flung open the back door and ran out to meet him. She threw her arms around him without waiting to see if he'd come to get his things and say goodbye, or if he'd come to stay.

"I missed you!" she said, pulling his head down to kiss him. His strong arms wrapped around her and he kissed her passionately, and it was then she was certain he hadn't come home to tell her goodbye. At least not yet.

He picked her up and carried her into the house, still kissing her. He kicked the back door closed behind him and suddenly her longing for him changed to an urgent desire for total intimacy, the union of hearts, as well as bodies.

Mike set her feet on the floor and raised his head. "Where's Jessie?"

"Asleep," Savannah said, pulling him back for her kiss, while she tugged loose his tie and unbuttoned his shirt. Mike unfastened her skirt and twisted free the buttons on her blouse. In minutes, clothes were strewn aside, and he leaned back against the door, picking her up again.

Savannah locked her legs around his strong body as he lowered her onto his thick shaft. They moved wildly. She wanted him beyond all else. She clung to his shoulders as urgency intensified into frenzy. Mike raised his head. "Savannah, I love you!"

Dimly she heard his words over her roaring pulse, but she was immersed in a raging need.

"Mike!" she cried later. "Mike, I want you!"

Words were gone as she exploded over a brink and rapture replaced need. While she clung to him, she felt his release, and then slowly they drifted back to awareness. He kissed her long and hard, lowering her to her feet.

"Let's go up to bed," she murmured, nuzzling his neck, her cheek tickled by the faint stubble of his beard.

When he framed her face with his hands, she looked up into his dark-brown eyes.

"I love you," he declared firmly.

"Oh, Mike!" Her heart pounded. "I love you and I've missed you. I don't care about Troy or the firm. They're not important. You're all—"

His mouth covered hers so hungrily that she trembled. Leaving their clothes behind, he carried her up to the shower, which they shared. Then when he had a towel around his middle and she had pulled on a terry robe, he headed for the bathroom door.

"I'll be right back. Don't go away," he said.

She laughed and held out her hands. "Where would I go?"

He smiled and left, and she began to blow-dry her hair. In minutes, he was back. He turned off the dryer and took it from her hands to set it down, then led her into their bedroom.

"Let's talk while we have a chance before Jessie wakes up," he said solemnly. She nodded as he moved to the small sofa and sat, pulling her down on his lap. He held out his hand. "I got this for you."

A small, black-velvet box nestled in the palm of his hand. As she took it, Savannah looked at him questioningly, then opened the lid. Nestled inside was a sapphire-and-diamond ring.

"Oh, Mike, it's beautiful!" Savannah gasped.

He took the ring from the box and held her right hand. "I know you have a ring from your parents that you wear, but I thought this ring would go with it."

"I love it!" She slipped off the gold ring with diamonds from her parents and slipped on the diamond-and-sapphire ring. "I may have the other ring made into a pendant. This is beautiful and I want to wear it all by itself."

"I gave you a wedding and an engagement ring when we married, but this ring is a ring of love, Savannah."

She looked into his eyes and put her arms around his neck to kiss him, her heart pounding wildly with joy. "Thank you and I love you and I'm so glad you're home!" she cried, tears of joy streaming down her cheeks.

"Hey, you're crying!"

"I'm happy!"

"So am I," he said around kisses, and then he shifted, pushing her gently down on the sofa and moving over her. His towel fell away, and in minutes he had peeled away Savannah's robe, and they made love again with just as much urgency as before.

Afterward, when they lay in each other's arms, Savannah looked again at her new ring. "I was scared you weren't coming back."

"I couldn't stand being away, but I had to go away so I could think clearly about our future. I can't think about anything when I'm near you."

"Ha! That's not so," she said, and he nuzzled her neck.

"Are we going to argue?"

"No!" She tightened her arms around him and smiled at him, and he smiled back at her. Jessie's cries came over the intercom and Mike got up.

"I've missed her. Let me get her," he said, fastening the towel around his middle again.

Savannah's gaze raked over him and she smiled with contentment and joy as she sat up to gather her clothes.

They were busy dressing and busy with Jessie, and it wasn't until after Jessie was in bed that night that Mike rejoined Savannah in the upstairs family room. He sat down to face her, gazing at her solemnly. "There's one issue we haven't discussed."

"Troy, and I don't care. Do what you want. He's not worth jeopardizing my marriage."

"I did do something," Mike said, going to get his briefcase and returning with pictures. "Here's the new firm," he said, handing snapshots to Savannah.

She looked at an elegant redbrick building with ornate white columns and professional landscaping.

"There's obviously money in it," she said. "You told me an ambulance chaser and the others didn't have big practices."

"That's right," Mike replied solemnly. "Savannah, Troy owns that building and the land."

Her mouth dropped open and she stared at one of the pictures in shock. Frowning, she looked up at Mike. "But why? We have a good practice. Why would he do this?"

"My first thought was to get back at you for not dating him."

"Surely not. We were never serious."

"Maybe *you* weren't."

"You said 'first thought.' What was your second thought?"

"I did some checking. Troy's lifestyle, which was never bad, has improved enormously in the last year. I think you should bring in an outside accountant and have an audit done on your books."

She started to protest and then remembered their argument before and how wrong she had been about Troy. She nodded. "I'll do it," she said.

"Good," Mike replied, a gleam entering his eyes. "So for now, we're through with Troy and can get back to being Mr. and Mrs. Remington. Come here," Mike said, pulling her onto his lap.

Two weeks later, the accountant presented his results to Savannah. Two days after that, she made another appointment to meet with him in her office. She had asked Mike to be present, so at ten o'clock that morning, the three were seated in Savannah's office. She called Troy to join them.

Troy sauntered into the office and looked at the three of them. His eyes narrowed when he saw Mike.

"Troy, I want you to meet Dwight Eaton, accountant," Savannah said.

The moment she said "accountant," Troy looked at Savannah questioningly.

"Have a seat, Troy," she said, and as soon as he had pulled a chair into their circle, she continued. "I think we should hear from Dwight first."

As Dwight Eaton read the sums of money that Troy had in billable hours from clients, yet unaccounted for in the firm, Troy jumped to his feet. "Savannah, this is a damned witch hunt! I need an attorney. I'm not going to listen to this."

"You can listen with your attorney," Mike said, standing, too. "It's already been turned over to the police, and charges of embezzlement are going to be filed."

"Dammit, this is all because of you," Troy snarled. He suddenly took a swing at Mike, who ducked and came back with a punch that connected with Troy's jaw, sending him reeling. Savannah called the police while Dwight Eaton grabbed his books and scrambled out of the way.

Troy came right back at Mike, lunging at him, but Mike caught him and flipped him over on his back onto the floor.

"Give it up!" Mike snapped. "You're going to jail."

Troy came to his feet, reaching into his pocket, but again Mike was faster and had Troy's arm twisted behind his back while he patted Troy's pockets and removed a pistol. Savannah gasped.

"Savannah, you and Dwight go in the other room," Mike ordered. "I'll wait here with Troy for the police."

Sirens wailed in the distance, and in minutes Troy was taken away in handcuffs as Mike stood beside Savannah with his arm around her shoulders.

As Troy was led out, he turned to glare at Savannah. "You bitch—"

Mike stepped in front of Savannah, but a policeman

pushed against Mike's chest. "Just get back, Colonel," the policeman said quietly. Mike did so, pulling Savannah close to his side.

Everyone in the firm was gathered in the lobby watching the proceedings, and Savannah turned to introduce the accountant and explain what had happened. Liz Fenton paled and blinked.

"I've been dating Troy for a year now," she said. She shook her head and turned to go to her office.

"I think we'll close up here for the day," Savannah announced. "All of you take the rest of the day off."

Everyone scattered, and within minutes Mike was driving Savannah toward Stallion Pass.

"I hate all this," Savannah said.

"You didn't cause it, so don't feel sorry for him. He's been embezzling funds for more than a year now."

"I don't feel sorry for him, I just don't like it. And I still can't understand why he did it."

"Just greed. And maybe a little wanting to get back at you for not dating him. Pretty basic reasons."

"He was well-off. He didn't need to steal."

"Some people always want more. At least the uncertainty is over. Now you can get on with your life."

Epilogue

Saturday night after hours of lovemaking, Savannah lay on a blanket on a sandy beach, pressed up against Mike. He lay on his side with his head propped on his elbow as he looked down at her and ran his fingers through her hair.

They could hear the soft lap of waves on the shore, and Savannah could see the white streak of moonlight reflected across the dark waters of the ocean.

"This is perfect," she said, stroking Mike's bare chest.

"A delayed honeymoon is better than no honeymoon."

"A delayed honeymoon is wonderful. Our own island—I love it."

"I can keep you out here nude all the next week, and there's no one to see anything because we've got this tropical island rented for another week and the place is stocked with enough food for a month."

"Besides my new husband being such an expert fisherman. This is great, Mike," she said, running her hands over him, touching scars lightly and glad he was no longer in the military. "Now, I'm not going to run around nude twenty-four hours a day."

"We'll see."

"Should we call home again and check on Jessie?" she asked, trailing her hand over his bare hip, down over his thigh.

"She's fine and you talked to your folks this afternoon."

"So you like the security business?"

"Yes. It's interesting. I prefer working with companies on industrial security and not jobs like the one for you and finding Wyatt's horses. I hope I don't have to search for stolen livestock ever again."

"Well, you got the white stallion and now you're in love."

"You'll never, ever convince me that it's because I own that horse."

"Well, you're the fourth guy and all of you are married."

"We would have been, anyway," he said, brushing a kiss across her temple. "You and I were married before I had the horse."

"But we weren't in love," she argued.

"Am I going to spend half of the rest of my life trying to win arguments?" he teased.

"Maybe, but the other half of your life will make up for it," she answered, and he laughed.

"Savannah, you know we have well over a million dollars in that inheritance. You could retire from the firm, get someone else to run it and stay home with little Jessie."

Savannah ran her finger along his jaw. "Maybe if you would give me a real incentive—like having another baby. Now with two—"

"Damn," he said, falling back on the blanket. "I'm just getting accustomed to the idea of parenthood and one baby. Now you're talking about two!"

She turned on her side to look down at him. "You're not up for another baby," she said, trailing kisses over his chest and then raising her head to look at him while she caressed his thigh.

He pushed her down again, moving over her. "I'm up for it," he said in a husky voice. "Just remember, it was your idea."

They both laughed and he pulled her close to kiss her. Savannah wrapped her arms around his neck and held him tightly, her heart pounding with a joy she had never expected to find, but now it was here because of one man who had walked into her office and into her life and her heart. She loved him and knew she would love him always.

*   *   *   *   *

Sara's tantalizing tales of these Texas Knights continue in Intimate Moments with

BRING ON THE NIGHT

Jonah Whitewolf has come to Stallion Pass to claim his inheritance—he never expected to come face-to-face with his ex-wife, Kate, and the son he had never known. Now Jonah must find a way to claim this family as his own, even if he must risk his own life to protect them.

Coming in June 2004
only from Silhouette Books.

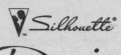

Reader favorite

Sara Orwig

**continues her popular
cross-line miniseries**

STALLION PASS:

TEXAS KNIGHTS

**Where the only cure for those hot and sultry
Lone Star days are some sexy-as-all-get-out
Texas Knights!**

**Don't miss this steamy round-up
of mouth-watering cowboys!**

SHUT UP AND KISS ME
(Silhouette Desire #1581, on-sale May 2004)

BRING ON THE NIGHT
(Silhouette Intimate Moments #1298, on-sale June 2004)

STANDING OUTSIDE THE FIRE
(Silhouette Desire #1594, on-sale July 2004)

Available at your favorite retail outlet.

eHARLEQUIN.com

For **FREE online reading,** visit
www.eHarlequin.com now and enjoy:

Online Reads
Read **Daily** and **Weekly** chapters from
our Internet-exclusive stories by your
favorite authors.

Red-Hot Reads
Turn up the heat with one of our more
sensual online stories!

Interactive Novels
Cast your vote to help decide how these
stories unfold…then stay tuned!

Quick Reads
For shorter romantic reads, try our
collection of Poems, Toasts, & More!

Online Read Library
Miss one of our online reads?
Come here to catch up!

Reading Groups
Discuss, share and rave with other
community members!

For great reading online,
visit www.eHarlequin.com today!

INTONL

If you enjoyed what you just read,
then we've got an offer you can't resist!

Take 2 bestselling love stories FREE!

Plus get a FREE surprise gift!

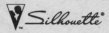
Silhouette®

INTIMATE MOMENTS™

From reader favorite
SARA ORWIG

Bring on the Night

(Silhouette Intimate Moments, #1298)

With a ranch in Stallion Pass, Jonah Whitewolf
inherited a mysterious danger—a threatening
enemy with a vendetta against him. When he
runs into his ex-wife, Kate Valentini, in town,
he comes face-to-face with the secret she's kept—
the son he never knew. With the truth revealed,
Jonah must put his life in peril to protect his
ranch and his family from jeopardy. But can he
face the greatest risk of all and give himself up
to love a second time around?

STALLION PASS: TEXAS KNIGHTS

*Where the only cure for those hot and sultry
Lone Star Days are some sexy-as-all-get-out
Texas Knights!*

Available June 2004 at your favorite retail outlet.

COMING NEXT MONTH

#1585 CHALLENGED BY THE SHEIKH—Kristi Gold
Dynasties: The Danforths

Hotshot workaholic Imogene Danforth was up for a promotion, and only her inability to ride a horse was standing in her way. Sheikh Raf Shakir had vowed to train her on one of his prized Arabians…provided she stay at his ranch. But what was Raf truly training Imogene to be: a wonderful rider or his new bed partner?

#1586 THE BRIDE TAMER—Ann Major

Forced to rely on her wealthy in-laws, Vivian Escobar never dreamed she'd meet a man as devastatingly sexy as Cash McRay—a man who was set to marry her sister-in-law but who only had eyes for Vivian. Dare they act on the passion between them? For their secret affair might very well destroy a family….

#1587 MISTRESS MINDED—Katherine Garbera
King of Hearts

With a lucrative contract on the line, powerful executive Adam Powell offered his sweet assistant the deal of a lifetime—pretend to be his mistress until the deal was sealed. Jayne Montrose was no fool; she knew this was the perfect opportunity to finally get into Adam's bed…and into his heart!

#1588 WILD IN THE MOONLIGHT—Jennifer Greene
The Scent of Lavender

She had a gift for making things grow…except when it came to relationships. Then Cameron Lachlan walked onto Violet Campbell's lavender farm and seduced her in the blink of an eye. Their passion burned hot and fast, but could their blossoming romance overcome the secret Violet kept?

#1589 HOLD ME TIGHT—Cait London
Heartbreakers

Desperate to hire the protective skills of Alexi Stepanov, Jessica Sterling found herself offering him anything he wanted. She never imagined his price would be so high, or that she would be so willing to give him everything he demanded…and more.

#1590 HOT CONTACT—Susan Crosby
Behind Closed Doors

On forced leave from the job that was essentially his entire life, Detective Joe Vicente was intrigued by P.I. Arianna Alvarado's request for his help. He agreed to aid her in her investigation, vowing not to become personally involved. But Joe soon realized that Arianna was a temptation he might not be able to resist.

SDCNM0504